The Launch Boys' Cruise in the Deerfoot

By
Edward S. Ellis

ILLUSTRATED BY
BURTON DONNEL HUGHES

ISBN-13:978-1496007964
ISBN-10:1496007964

THE BIG SHIP WAS STILL COMING TOWARD HIM

CONTENTS

CHAPTER I. BETWEEN TWO FIRES 4

CHAPTER II. LIVELY TIMES 11

CHAPTER III. MIKE MURPHY 18

CHAPTER IV. A LOAN TO CAPTAIN LANDON 26

CHAPTER V. A MOTOR BOAT 35

CHAPTER VI. CAPTAIN AND CREW 40

CHAPTER VII. ONE AUGUST DAY 49

CHAPTER VIII. A PASSING GLIMPSE 57

CHAPTER IX. NO MAN'S LAND 65

CHAPTER X. THE LURE OF GOLD 73

CHAPTER XI. A MISSING MOTOR BOAT 79

CHAPTER XII. IN THE TELEGRAPH OFFICE 87

CHAPTER XIII. A SLIGHT MISTAKE 96

CHAPTER XIV. A FRIEND IN NEED 104

CHAPTER XV. A GLIMPSE OF SOMETHING 113

CHAPTER XVI. ON BARTER ISLAND 120

CHAPTER XVII. THE MAN IN GRAY 128

CHAPTER XVIII. AT THE INLET 136

CHAPTER XIX. NOT NEAR EITHER BANK 144

CHAPTER XX. A DISAPPOINTMENT 152

CHAPTER XXI. A TELEGRAM 160

CHAPTER XXII. FOUND 168

CHAPTER XXIII. CAPTAIN AND MATE 176

CHAPTER XXIV. "THIS IS WHERE I STOP" 184

CHAPTER XXV. GOOD NEWS 191

CHAPTER XXVI. DISQUIETING NEWS 199

CHAPTER XXVII. AN ALARMING FACT 207

CHAPTER XXVIII. THE CRY ACROSS THE WATERS ... 215

CHAPTER XXIX. MAROONED 222

CHAPTER XXX. A NEW ENGLAND HOME COMING . 231

CHAPTER XXXI. THE MAN IN GRAY 239

CHAPTER I. Between Two Fires

I once heard the bravest officer I ever knew declare that the height of absurdity was for a person to boast that he did not know the meaning of fear. "Such a man is either a fool or the truth is not in him," was the terse expression of the gallant soldier.

Now it would have been hard to find a more courageous youth than Alvin Landon, who had just entered his seventeenth year, and yet he admits that on a certain soft moonlit night in summer he felt decidedly "creepy," and I believe you and I would have felt the same in his situation. He was walking homeward and had come to a stretch of pine forest that was no more than an eighth of a mile in length. The road was so direct that when you entered the wood you could see the opening at the farther side, where you came again upon meadows and cultivated fields. The highway was so broad that only a portion of it was shaded and there was no excuse for one losing his way even when the moon and stars failed to give light. All you had to do was to "keep in the middle of the road" and plod straight on.

But when the orb of night rode high in the sky and the course was marked as plainly as at midday, there was always the deep gloom on the right and left, into which the keenest eye could not penetrate. A boy's imagination was apt to people the obscurity with frightful creatures crouching and waiting for a chance to pounce upon him.

Alvin was a student in a preparatory school on the Hudson, where he was making ready for his admission to the United States Military Academy at West Point. The appointment had been guaranteed his father, a wealthy capitalist, by one of the Congressmen of his district, but nearly two years had to pass before the lad would be old enough to become a cadet, and pass the rigid mental and physical examination required of every one enrolled in the most admirable military institution in the world.

On this mild August night he was going home from the little cove where his motor boat nestled under the shed built for its protection. His chum Chester Haynes, about his own age, lived within a hundred yards of the shelter of the craft, so that it was always under his eye, when not dashing up the Kennebec or some of its tributaries, or cruising over the broad waters of Casco Bay. On their return from an all-day excursion, they reached Chester's home so late that Alvin stayed to supper. It was dark when he set out for his own home, a good half mile north, the last part of the walk leading through the odorous pines of which I have made mention.

The lad had no weapon, for he needed none. His father was opposed to the too free use of firearms by boys and insisted that when a lad found it necessary to carry a pistol for protection it was time for him to stay within doors where no one could harm him.

The youth was impatient because of a certain nervousness which came to him when he stepped into the pulseless gloom and saw far ahead the broad silvery door opening into the open country beyond.

"About all the Indians in this part of the world," he mused, yielding to a whimsical fancy, "are at Oldtown; the others are making baskets, bows and arrows, moccasins and trinkets to sell to summer visitors. There used to be bears and panthers and wolves and deer in Maine, but most of them are in the upper part. I shouldn't dare to shoot a buck or moose if he came plunging at me with antlers lowered, for it is the close season and a fellow can't satisfy the wardens by saying he had to shoot in self-defence. As for other kinds of wild animals, there's no use of thinking of them.

"I should be ashamed to let Chester know I felt creepy to-night, when I have been through these woods so often without a thought of anything wrong. But it does seem to me that some sort of mischief is brooding in the air—"

"Tu-whit-tu-whoo-oo!"

Alvin must have leaped a foot from the ground. He was sure he felt his cap rise several inches above his crown, with still an upward tendency. Then he softly laughed.

"Only a screech owl, but that hoot when you are not expecting it is startling enough to make a fellow jump. It seems to me nature might have given that bird a more cheerful voice, say like the thrush or nightingale. Then it would be pleasant to listen to his music after dark. I remember when I was a little codger and was coming home late one night, near Crow's Nest, one of those things began hooting right over my head and I didn't stop running till I tumbled through the gate. I think I have a little more sense now than in those days."

It did not add to his peace of mind when he glanced behind him to see a shadowy form coming toward him from the rear and keeping so close to the line of obscurity on his right that only a flitting glimpse of him was caught. Few situations are more nerve-racking than the discovery at night of an unknown person dogging your footsteps. He may be a friend or an enemy—more likely the latter—and you see only evil intent in his stealthy pursuit.

But Alvin's good sense quieted his fears and he resumed his course, still holding the middle of the road, alert and watchful.

"He can't mean any harm," he thought, "for everyone in this part of the country is a neighbor of the others. I shall be glad to have his company and will lag so that he will soon overtake me—hello!"

It was at this juncture that two ghost-like figures suddenly whisked across the road in front. They seemed to be in a hurry and acted as if they wished to escape observation—though why they should feel thus was more than Alvin could guess. It dawned upon him that he was between two fires.

"It's queer that so many strangers are abroad to-night, though they have as much right to tramp through the country as I."

At the time of learning the rather disquieting fact, young Landon had gone two-thirds of the way through the wood, so that the couple in front were near the open country. Striving to convince himself that he had no cause for misgiving, he still felt uneasy as he moved stealthily forward. He gave no thought to the one behind, for it was easy to avoid him. His interest centered upon the two in front, with whom he was quite sure to come in contact. They were no longer in sight, but whether they were walking in the broad ribbon of shadow at the side of the highway, or awaiting his approach, was impossible to tell.

He stopped and listened. The one dismal hoot of the owl seemed to have satisfied the bird, which remained silent. The straining ear failed to catch the slightest footfall. Recalling the feathery dust upon which he was stepping, Alvin knew that no one could hear his footfalls.

For the first time, he now left the band of illumination, moving into the darkness on his left. There he could be invisible to everyone not less than four or five paces away.

"If they don't wish me to see them, there's no reason why they should see me," was the thought which impelled him. Gradually he slackened his pace until he stood still. Then with all his senses keyed to a high tension he did some hard thinking. Despite his ridicule of his own fears, he could not shake off the suspicion that mischief was brooding over him. The two men in front and the third at the rear belonged to the same party.

"They mean to rob me," muttered Alvin, compressing his lips.

The belief seemed reasonable, for he was worthy of the attention of one or more yeggmen. He carried a gold watch, the gift of his father, a valuable pin in his scarf, a present from his mother, and always had a generous amount of money with him. Many a youth in his situation would have meekly surrendered his property upon the demand of a company of criminals against whom it was impossible to prevail, but our young friend was made of sterner stuff. He would not yield so long as he could fight, and his bosom burned with righteous anger at the thought that such an outrage was possible in these later days.

All the same, he was too sensible to invite a physical encounter so long as there was a good chance of avoiding it. The wisest thing to do was to step noiselessly in among the pines at his side, pick his way for a few rods, and then wait for the danger to pass; or he could continue to steal forward, shaping his course so as to reach the open country, so far to one side of the highway that no one would see him.

You will smile when I tell you why Alvin Landon did not follow this plan.

"They may suspect what I'm doing and sneak along the edge of the wood to catch me as I come out. Then I'll have to run for it, and I'll be hanged if I'll run from all the yeggmen in the State of Maine!"

He listened intensely, not stirring a muscle for several minutes. Once he fancied he heard a faint rustling a little way behind him, but it might have been a falling leaf. At the front the silence was like that of the tomb.

"They're waiting for me. Very well!"

Instead of keeping within the darkness, he stepped back into the middle of the road and strode forward with his usual pace. He did not carry so much as a cane or broken limb with which to defend himself. All at once he began whistling that popular college air, "When I saw Sweet Nellie Home." He would not admit to himself that it was because he felt the slightest fear, but somehow or other, the music seemed to take the place of a companion. He began to suspect that it might not be so bad after all for a frightened lad thus to cheer himself when picking his course through a dark reach of woods.

"At any rate it can't tell them where I am, for all of them already know it," was his conclusion.

CHAPTER II. Lively Times

As Alvin Landon drew near the open country he gave his thoughts wholly to the two strangers in front, ceasing to look back or listen for the one at the rear. The keen eyes strove to penetrate the silent gloom on his right and left, but they saw nothing. Probably fifty feet intervened between him and the full flood of moonlight, when, with more startling effect than that caused by the hooting of the owl, a sepulchral voice sounded through the stillness:

"Hold on there, pard!"

It was purely instinctive on the part of the youth that he made a bound forward and dashed off on a dead run. Not until he burst into the bright illumination did he awaken to the fact that he was doing the very opposite of what he intended and actually playing the coward. The fact that his natural courage had come back was proved at the same moment of his abrupt stoppage, for the sharp report of a pistol rang out from directly behind him. The space was so short that it was evident the shot had been fired not to harm him, but to check his flight.

At the moment of halting, he whirled around and saw a youth who could have been no older than himself charging impetuously upon him. Alvin's halt was so instant and so unexpected on the part of his pursuer that they would have collided but for the fugitive's fist, which shot out and landed with full force upon the face of the other. Alvin knew how to strike hard, and the energy which he threw into the effort was intensified by the swift approach of his assailant.

No blow could have been more effective. With a grunt, his foe tumbled headlong, flapped over on his back and lay as if dead. Had he been the only enemy, the combat would have ended then and there, for never was an antagonist knocked out more emphatically, but his companion now dashed into the fray.

He was somewhat older than the one who had come to grief, but still lacked full maturity. Too cautious to make the mistake of the other, he checked himself while just beyond the fist that had done such admirable work. With an oath he shouted:

"I'll teach you how to kill my pal."

"I don't need any teaching; come on and I'll serve you the same way," replied Alvin, eager for the attack to be made.

His opponent came on. He had learned from the rashness of his partner, for after putting up his hands, like a professional pugilist, he began feinting and circling about Alvin, in the search for an inviting opening. The latter did not forget the instruction he had received from Professor Donovan and stood on his guard, equally vigilant for an advantage.

The elder had made a complete circle about Alvin, who turned as on a pivot to meet his attack, and was just quick enough to parry the vicious blow launched at him, but not quick enough to counter effectively. The next instant the fist of the taller fellow came in contact with the chest of Alvin, who was driven back several paces. His foe attempted to follow it up, but was staggered by a facer delivered straight and true. Then our young friend in turn pressed the other, who, bewildered by the rapidity and fierceness of the assault, made a rush to clinch.

Nothing could have suited Alvin better and he met the effort with a storm of furious blows. The chief one was aimed at the chin, and had it landed the result would have been a knockout, but it was a trifle short. Determined not to be denied, Alvin pressed on with all the power at his command. "Keep cool and strike straight," was the motto of his instructor at the gymnasium, and though he was enraged he heeded the wise advice.

Nearly a score of blows were exchanged with such rapidity that a spectator could not have kept track of them, and then Alvin "got there." The thud was followed by an almost complete somersault of the victim. The master was prompted to push his success by attacking his enemy before he could rise, but another law flashed upon Alvin. "Never strike a man when he is down," a chivalrous policy when the rules of the game govern both contestants. It was doubtful whether Alvin would have received similar consideration had the situation been reversed, but he could not feel sure of that until the proof was given. He therefore calmly waited for the other to rise, when he would be upon him like a tiger.

A minute or two passed before the fallen one recovered enough to begin climbing to his feet. He could have risen sooner, but deceived his conqueror by feigning weakness and fumbled aimlessly about as if too groggy to get his bearings. But he was helping in a treacherous trick.

As Alvin stood, his back was toward the first miscreant, who recovered from his stupor while his companion still lay on the ground. Our young friend gave no thought to the one, whom he believed to be out of the affair altogether.

The same young man, however, gave quick thought to him. Bounding to his feet he sneaked up unseen and struck a blow that drove Alvin forward so violently that he had to make a leap over the second assailant to avoid falling upon him. It was a wonder that he was not struck down senseless. As it was, he was partially stunned, but rallied in a flash.

Now it would have been sensible and no disgrace to the heroic lad, when he found himself confronted by two muscular and enraged youths, to dash at full speed for home. But he did nothing of the kind.

"Come on, both of you!" he called out. "I'm not afraid and you haven't got me yet!"

It would be a pleasure to record that our young friend defeated the couple, but such a triumph in the nature of things was impossible. Either of them would have given him all he could do, and the two united were sure to overcome him. With his stubborn resolve to have it out with them he must have suffered but for an unexpected turn of events.

You remember that a third stranger was approaching from the other direction. In the hurricane rush of the fight, Alvin forgot about him, but he now arrived and threw himself with a vengeance into the affray. His bursting upon the scene convinced the lone defender that the time had come to show his ability as a sprinter. While quite ready to oppose two, he knew he could not stand up against three. Before he started, however, he saw with a thrill that the new arrival had attacked with unrestrainable fierceness the one who had just struck Alvin. In other words, instead of being an enemy he was a much-needed ally.

This stranger did not utter a word at first, but attended strictly to business, and that he was a master of it was proved by his first blow, which sent the fellow staggering backward finally falling with his heels kicking toward the orb of night. There was no thought of chivalry on the part of the conquerer, who landed again as he was climbing to his feet.

"Let up!" protested the victim. "Do you want to kill a fellow?"

"Begorrah, ye guessed it right the fust time!" was the reply of the friend, who turned to Alvin:

"If ye'll smash that spalpeen I'll be attending to the same wid this one."

The slight diversion was enough to give the dazed victim on the ground time to come to his feet, when he turned and was off like a deer in the direction whence had come his conqueror. Determined not to be despoiled of his victory, the Irish lad—as his accent showed him to be—pursued at the highest bent of speed. But his short legs were not equal to the task, and the terrified assailant made such excellent time that a few minutes sufficed to carry him beyond all danger. The "broth of a boy" would not give up at first. The two held their places in the middle of the highway, so that both were in plain sight, with the fugitive steadily drawing away.

"Howld on, ye spalpeen!" shouted the pursuer. "I'm not through wid ye!"

But he who fled was glad enough to be through with the business, and kept up his desperate flight until the other ceased and turned back to learn how matters were going with the friend to whose aid he had rushed.

A somewhat similar story was to be told of the second miscreant, who had seized the chance to take to flight in the opposite direction. In this case, the fleet footed Alvin proved the superior in speed and within a hundred yards overtook him. The moment he was within reach he let drive and his fist landed in the back of the other's neck. Inasmuch as he was going at his highest speed and the blow sent his head and shoulders forward with additional swiftness, the inevitable result was that he fell, his face plowing the dirt and his hat flying a dozen feet from him.

Before he could rise, Alvin was upon him. The fellow threw up his hands to protect his countenance and whined:

"Please don't hit me again! I'm half killed now!"

The cringing appeal changed Alvin's indignation to disgusted pity. He unclenched his fingers and dropped his hands.

"Get up! I won't hit you, though you deserve it."

His victim seemed to be in doubt and slowly came to his feet still whining:

"We didn't know it was you; it was a mistake."

"It does look that way," was the grim comment of Alvin. "Get up, I say; you have nothing to fear from me."

The fellow was in doubt. He slowly rose, but the instant he stood erect, he was off again as if propelled from a catapult. Alvin, instead of pursuing and overtaking him, stood still and laughed.

"Come back and get your hat!" he shouted, but the fugitive did not abate his speed and made the dust fly until he vanished in the moonlight.

Yielding to an impulse, Alvin walked to where the headgear lay and picked it up. It was a valuable chip hat, such as is fashionable in summer in all parts of the country. The captor was wondering whether it contained the fellow's name. The moonlight was not strong enough for him to see distinctly, and, bringing out his rubber safe from his hip pocket, he struck a match to aid in the scrutiny.

CHAPTER III. Mike Murphy

Holding the tiny flicker of flame in the hollow of the hat, Alvin saw in fancy gilt letters, pasted on the silk lining, the following:

"NOXON O"

"That's a queer name," he reflected. "I never heard anything like it."

"Do ye know ye're holding the same upside down?"

The Irish lad, panting from his exertion in running, stood grinning at Alvin's elbow. "'Spose ye turns the hat round so as to revarse the same."

Alvin did so and then read "O NOXON."

"It's the oddest name I ever saw, for 'NOXON' reads the same upside down and backwards—Ugh!"

Seized with a sudden loathing, he sent the hat skimming a dozen feet away. His feeling was as if he had grasped a serpent. Then he turned and impulsively offered his hand to the Irish lad.

"Shake! You were a friend in need."

"It's mesilf that's under deep obligations to yersilf."

"How do you make that out?"

"Didn't ye give me the finest chance for a shindy that I've had since I lift Tipperary? I haven't had so much fun since Pat Geoghaghan almost whaled the life out of me at home."

"Who are you?"

"Mike Murphy, at your sarvice."

And the grinning lad lifted his straw hat and bowed with the grace of a crusader.

"Where do you live?"

"Up the road a wee bit, wid me father and mither."

"Are you the son of Pat Murphy?" asked the astonished Alvin.

"He has the honor, according to his own story, of being me dad."

"Why, he's father's caretaker. I remember he told me some time ago that he had a boy seventeen years old that he had sent word to in Ireland to come over and join him. And you are he! Why, I'm so glad I should like to shake hands with you again."

"I'm nothing loath, but I say that hat ye threw away is more of the fashion in this part of the wurruld than in Tipperary, and if ye have no objections I'll make a trade."

And the Irish lad walked to where the headgear lay, picked it up and pulled it on his crown.

"It's a parfect fit—as the tramp said when he bounced around the kind leddy's yard—don't I look swaat in the same?"

Alvin could not help laughing outright, for the hat was at least a size too small for the proud new owner, and perched on his crown made his appearance more comical than it had been formed by nature.

"I knew ye would be plased, as me uncle said when the docther towld him he would be able to handle his shillaleh inside of a waak and meet his engagement with Dennis O'Shaugnessey at Donnybrook fair. Me dad tached me always to be honest."

To prove which Mike laid down his battered straw hat beside the road, where the seeker of the better headgear would have no trouble in finding it. "And if it's all the same, Alvin, we'll adjourn to our home, for I'm so hungry I could ate me own grandmither."

"How did you know my name?" asked the surprised Alvin.

"Arrah, now, hasn't me dad and mither been writing me since they moved into this part of the wurruld and spaking of yersilf? It was yer telling me that me dad was your dad's caretaker that towld the rist. Ef I had known it was yersilf I would have hit that spalpeen harder."

"You did well as it was. But I say, Mike, when did you arrive in Maine?"

"Only three days since. Having had directions from me dad, as soon as I got ashore in New York I made fur the railway station, where I wint to slaap in the cars and woke up in Portland. Thar I had time to ate breakfast and ride in the train to Bath, where I meant to board the steamboat Gardiner. I had half a minute to sprint down the hill to the wharf, but the time was up before I got there and the men pulled in the plank when I was twinty faat away. I'm told the Captain niver tarries ten seconds for anybody."

"That's true," replied Alvin, "for I have seen him steam away when by waiting half a minute he would have gained five or six passengers."

"So I had to tarry for the other steamer, which lift me off at Southport, and I walked the rist of the way to the home of me parents. I mind dad towld me the same was four or five miles, but I think it was six hundred full. I found me parents yesterday."

"I remember now that your father said he expected you about this time, but it had slipped my mind, and having been away all day I had no chance to learn of your coming. But I can tell you, Mike, I'm mighty glad to know you."

"The same to yersilf," was the hearty response of the Irish lad. In fact, considering the circumstances in which the two met, to say nothing of their congenial dispositions, nothing was more natural than that they should form a strong liking for each other. They walked side by side, sometimes in the dusty road or over the well-marked path on the right or left, and talking of everything that came into their minds.

"How was it you happened to be passing over this road to-night when I found myself in so great need of you?" asked Alvin.

"Me dad sint me this noon down to Cape Newagen to inquire for some letters he didn't ixpect, and then to keep on to Squirrel Island and buy him a pound of 'bacca and to be sure to walk all the way and be back in time for supper, which I much fear me I sha'n't be able to do."

"How did you make out?" asked the amused Alvin.

"As well as might be ixpected," gravely replied Mike, "being there ain't any store at Cape Newagen and I should have to walk under water for near two miles or swim to Squirrel Island, barring the fact that I can't swim a stroke to save me life."

"What did your father mean by sending you on such a fool errand?"

Mike chuckled.

"It was a joke on me. I've tried to break him of the habit, but he can't help indulging in the same whin he gits the chance. He was so glad to have me wid him that he found an excuse for whaling me afore last night and then played this trick on me."

"Didn't your mother tell you better?"

"Arrah, but she's worse nor him; she said I would enj'y the walk and I may say I did though I couldn't extind the same as far as they had planned for me. Can you suggist something I kin do, Alvin, by the which I can git aven wid the owld folks fur the fun they've had wid me?"

"I am not able to think of anything just now."

"Ah, I have it!" broke in the Irish youth, snapping his fingers. "It has been the rule all me life that whin I got into a fight I must report the whole sarcumstances of the same to dad. If I licked the other chap, it was all right and he or mither give me an extra pratie at dinner, but if I was bested, then dad made himself tired using his strap over me back and legs. He's in high favor of me exercising my fists on others, but never will agraa that I don't do a hanus wrong when I git licked. 'It's such a bad habit,' he explains, that it's his dooty to whale it out of me."

"What has your fight to-night to do with playing a joke on him?"

"Why, don't you see that I'll make him think fur a time that it was mesilf that was knocked skyhigh, and after he's lambasted me till he can't do so any more, and I kin hardly stand, you and me will tell him the truth."

"Where will be the joke in that? It seems to me it will be wholly on you."

"Don't ye observe that he and mither will feel so bad whin they find how they have aboosed me that they'll give me two praties instid of one and then I'll have the laugh on them."

"It takes an Irishman or Irish boy to think up such a joke as that," was the comment of Alvin, as the two just then came in sight of the small log structure in which Pat Murphy and his wife made their home, while a light twinkled beyond from the windows of the larger building, where Alvin lived with his parents during the summer. A half mile to the south toward Cape Newagen was the more moderate dwelling, during the sultry season, of Chester Haynes, his chum from whom he had parted an hour or two previous to making the acquaintance of Mike Murphy. As they drew near the structure, Mike stepped in front and opened the door, with Alvin at his heels. Within, sat the father calmly smoking his pipe, while his tall, muscular but pleasant-faced wife by the table in the middle of the room with spectacles on her nose was busily sewing. The light was acetylene, furnished from the same source that supplied the large bungalow only a few paces distant.

"Good evening, Pat, and the top of the evening to you, Mrs. Murphy. You see I have brought Mike safely home to you."

Alvin was a favorite with the couple, who warmly greeted him. The boy was fond of calling at the humble dwelling and chatting with the two. Sometimes he took a meal with them, insisting that the food was much better than was provided by the professional chef in his own home. No surer means of reaching the heart of the honest woman could have been thought of, and though she insisted that the lad had kissed the blarney stone, she was none the less pleased by his kind words.

"Mither, I'm that near starved," said Mike, dropping into the nearest chair, "that I should perish if I had a dozen more paces to walk."

"Yer supper has been waiting for more than an hour, and if ye'll pass into the kitchen ye may eat your fill."

Mike took a step in the direction, but was halted by his father.

"Where is the 'bacca I ordered ye to bring from Squirrel Island?"

"They're out of the kind ye smoke, dad, and that which the storekeeper showed me was that poor I wouldn't have anything to do wid the same."

"And the litters at Cape Newagen?"

"They're expicting the one from King George that ye were looking fur, but it won't be in until the next steamer."

CHAPTER IV. A Loan to Captain Landon

The elder Murphy looked at his son with a quizzical expression and then glanced at the hat which had been hung on a peg behind the door.

"And where did ye get that?"

"Traded me owld one for it, but I had to go through a foight before the ither chap would give his consint."

The father's face brightened.

"So ye've been in anither foight, have ye, and only well landed in Ameriky."

"I niver had a foiner one," replied the son, still standing in the open door which led to the kitchen; "it makes me heart glad when I think of the same."

"And which licked?"

Mike was quick to seize the opportunity for which he was waiting. With a downcast expression, he humbly asked:

"Do ye expict me to win ivery time, dad?"

"Av coorse I do; haven't I trained ye up to that shtyle of fightin'?"

"Suppose, dad, the ither chap is bigger and stronger—what do ye ixpict of me?"

"Ye know yoursilf what to expict when ye disgraces the name of Murphy."

Laying his pipe on the table beside which his wife was sitting, the parent grimly rose and moved toward the door on the other side of the room that opened into the small apartment where the firewood was stored from wetting by rain. The three knew the meaning of the movement: he was seeking the heavy strap that was looped over a big spike. He had brought it from Tipperary two years before and must have kept it against the coming of his heir, knowing he would have use for it.

"Have done wid yer supper," he said to Mike, "and after the same, I'll do me dooty by ye."

The grinning lad was still standing in the kitchen door. The action of his father turned his back toward the youth, who winked at Alvin, stepped across the threshold and sat down at the end of the table where he was in sight, but the greater portion of the table itself was hidden.

Although the moonlight had given the visitor a good view of his young friend, the glow of the lamp now showed his face and features with the distinctness of midday. Alvin was sure he had never seen so homely a youth. The countenance was broad and covered with so many freckles that they showed on the tips of his large ears. The nose was an emphatic pug, and the mouth wide and filled with large white teeth, upon which no dentist could have found a pin speck. His short hair was the color of a well burned brick, stood straight up from the crown and projected like quills from the sides of his head, his complexion being of the same hue as the hair.

Although of stocky build, being hardly as tall as Alvin, the frame of the Irish youth was a model of strength and grace. There were few of his age who in a rough and tumble bout could hold their own with him. The night being sultry, he wore no coat or waistcoat, but the shirt, guiltless of tie, was clean, as were the trousers supported by a belt encircling the sturdy waist. His dusty tan shoes were neatly tied and the yellow socks which matched them could not have been less soiled.

The best "feature" about Mike Murphy was his good nature. His spirits were irrepressible, and he was always ready with quip and wit. Looking into the broad shining face one was reminded of the remark made about Abraham Lincoln: he was so homely that he crossed the line and became handsome.

Alvin's chair being near the front door with Mike in plain sight, he kept his eyes upon him for a minute or two. He saw him reach his fork across the table and bring a huge baked potato to his plate. He twisted it apart in the middle so as to expose the flaky whiteness and then snapped the fingers of both hands at his sides. With a grin he looked at Alvin and asked:

"Do ye know what's the hottest thing in the wurruld?"

"How about a live coal of fire?"

"Arrah, now, it's the inside of a baked pratie; a coal of fire is a cooling breeze alongside the same. Be the same towken, can ye tell me the cowldest thing on airth?"

"A piece of ice will do very well."

"Ye're off: it's the handle of a pitchfork on a frosty mornin'; if ye don't belave it try the expirimint for yersilf. But I must attind to plaisure, as me cousin said whin he grabbed his shillaleh and attacked his loved brother."

Mike now gave his whole attention to the meal. When it is remembered that he was ravenously hungry and the provision bountiful, enough is said. His father came back into the sitting room, tossed the heavy strap on the stand, beside which his wife was still serenely sewing, picked up his pipe and by sucking vigorously upon it renewed the fire that had nearly gone out. He crossed his legs and slowly rocked to and fro, glancing hospitably at Alvin.

While the latter was greatly amused by what he had seen and heard, he was also distressed for his friend Mike, whose idea of a joke was unique. There could be no mistaking the meaning of his father's actions. The son was due for a sharp castigation and was certain to receive it unless the caller interposed with a truthful statement of the recent occurrence.

Alvin rose from his chair and stepping to the kitchen door, gently closed it. Mrs. Murphy looked up through her spectacles.

"I don't wonder that ye wants to shet out the noise Mike makes whin aiting, fur the same is scand'lous."

"It isn't that, but I don't wish him to hear what I say to you."

"Shall I tell him to hold a finger of aich hand in his ears while he's aiting?" asked the mother without a smile.

"He might find that inconvenient. Mike told you the truth when he said he was in a fight to-night."

"I don't doubt the same, but I demands to know why he 'lowed himself to git licked?" said the father, with no little heat.

"He wasn't licked: it was the other fellow who got the worst of it."

"Why, thin, did the spalpeen say it was himself that was bested?"

"Begging your pardon, Pat, he did not. He stated a general truth, which no one can deny, to the effect that a fellow like him takes a chance of being defeated now and then. Listen to my story."

Thereupon Alvin related the incidents with which you are familiar, adding:

"If it hadn't been for Mike's arrival and his brave fight in my behalf, I should have been badly beaten and robbed. The first wretch even fired a pistol during the rumpus."

"Did he kill aither of ye?" asked the startled father.

"The shot was not aimed at me or him, but was meant to scare me into stopping and giving up. If I had thought of it I should have taken the weapon from him and given it to Mike. Let me tell you," added Alvin impressively, "both of you ought to be proud of such a son as Mike."

"So we are," quietly remarked the mother, without looking up or checking her flying needle.

"There isn't a pluckier lad in the world. He came to my help like a whirlwind, and the way he sailed into the fellow who struck me from behind showed Mike to be a hero."

The father reached out and grasped the loop of leather lying on the stand. Rising to his feet he passed into the small room where the stove wood was piled and hung the strap again upon the metal peg. As he came back and resumed his seat he sighed. It looked as if he was disappointed.

"What do you intend to do with him, Pat?"

"Train him up in the way he should go. Whin the school opens at Southport he will attind there, and whin he's at home I'll find enough to kaap him out of mischief."

"School will not open until September, which is several weeks away. I want you to lend Mike to me until then."

Mrs. Murphy stopped her sewing for the moment and looked at their visitor. Her husband removed the pipe from his mouth and also stared at him.

"Lind him to ye!" he repeated. "And phwat would you do wid him?"

"You know father bought me a motor boat, which arrived a few days ago. Chester Haynes and I have had great fun cruising up the Kennebec and different bays and streams, and we are going to keep at it until we have to go home. We want Mike to join us and share our sport, just as long as Chester and I are in this part of the world. You won't refuse me the favor?"

It was evident that the parents were pleased with the request. The proud mother said:

"Mike is so gintle that he'll be a good companion for anyone."

"Yis; because of his gintleness," repeated the father grimly. "But it saams to me ye're too kind, Alvin; he won't be able to airn his kaap and the indulgence ye'll give him."

"Won't earn them! Why, we don't intend to hire him; it's the pleasure we shall have in the company of such a good fellow as Mike. Besides," added Alvin, lowering his voice, "I have a feeling that we're not through with those two fellows who attacked me to-night. Mike won't be satisfied until he has paid the one who ran away from him and left his hat behind."

"Ye're wilcome to the lad," assented his father, "and I take it as very good on yer part, which is what ivery one has a right to ixpict from yersilf and father."

"No blarneying, Pat," protested their caller. "I am obliged to you for granting my request, for the favor will be wholly given to us."

"Now it's yersilf that's blarneying," said Pat.

The kitchen door softly opened and the grinning, red-faced Mike came into the room and sat down near his young friend.

"I overheerd ivery word that was said, Captain, and it's Mike Murphy that's thankful for yer kindness. I'm wid ye to the ind."

The others laughed at the use of the title by the Irish youth, who explained:

"Av coorse it's 'Captain Landon,' being that ye're the owner of the motor boat, as ye calls the same."

"And you shall be my first mate," said Alvin.

"Won't Chister, as ye name him, be jealous and indulge in mootiny?"

"No fear of that; we'll satisfy him by making him second mate, while all three will form the crew. And now I must bid you good night. I shall call for you as soon as we are through breakfast to-morrow morning."

With which our young friend went to his own home.

CHAPTER V. A Motor Boat

The first time you stepped aboard a motor boat you were impressed by the looks of the engine and the numerous appliances which when rightly handled drive the craft through the water at the rate of ten, fifteen, twenty and sometimes more miles an hour. You thought it would be hard to learn to manage the boat and know how to overcome the different kinds of trouble that are almost certain to arise. But the task, after all, is simple and with patience you can soon master it.

In the first place let us find out the principle which governs the smooth, swift progress of the structure. I shall be as brief and pointed as possible.

As a foundation, we need a good supply of clean, strained gasoline in the tank. Unless the fluid is free from all impurities it is likely to clog and interfere with the working of the machinery. The tank is so placed that its elevation is sufficient to cause the gasoline to flow by gravity through the pipe, which is connected by an automatic valve with the carburettor, admitting just enough to answer the purpose desired. As the gasoline is sprayed into the carburettor a quantity of air is drawn in from the outside. The two mingle and form a highly explosive gas. To start, you give the fly-wheel a rapid swing, which causes the piston to move downward. This action sucks the gaseous mixture into the cylinder through the inlet valve. The further movement of the fly-wheel causes the piston to move upward, compressing the gas into small volume. While the gas is thus compressed it is exploded by means of an electric spark. The violent expansion of the burning gas drives the piston downward with great force. The movement opens the exhaust valve, the burnt gases escape through the exhaust pipe and the fresh mixture is drawn in again to be compressed and exploded as before. If the engine has more than one cylinder the same process is repeated in each one. This is the operation which is continued so long as the supply of gasoline holds out.

In the steam engine the vapor acts alternately on each side of the piston head, but in motor boats and automobiles it acts only on one side. The speed with which this is done is amazing and the same may be said of the steam engine.

The swift rise and fall of the piston acting through the connecting rod turns the shaft directly below, which whirls the screw around at the stern. The electric spark that explodes the vapor is generated by a dry battery or by a magneto-electric machine driven by the motor itself. There is also the "make and break" spark, to which we need give no attention. The two ends of the wires in the spark plug which is screwed into the cylinder are separated by a space barely the twentieth part of an inch, across which the spark leaps, giving out an intensely hot flash.

You understand, of course, that I have given simply the principle and method of operation of the engine belonging to a motor boat. There are many parts that must operate smoothly and with the minimum of friction. Lubricating oil is as essential as gasoline; the ignition battery must be kept dry; you must know how to operate the reversing lever, to shut off, to start and to hold the desired speed. Except when racing or under some pressing necessity, the swiftest progress is rarely attained, for it is trying to all parts of the engine and consumes a good deal of fuel, which cannot be bought for a trifling price.

You would be confused by any attempt on my part to give a technical description of all the motor appliances, nor is there need to do so. If you have just bought a motor boat, you will be taught how to control and manage it by a practical instructor, and such instruction is better than pages of directions. To show the truth of what I have just said, I will quote a single paragraph from the description of the boat concerning which I shall have a good deal to say in the course of my story.

"The keel is of white oak, with specially bent elm frames. Planking of selected Laguna mahogany, finished thickness one-half inch, in narrow strakes and uniform seams, secured to frames by copper boat nails, riveted over copper washers, all fastenings being of bronze or copper to withstand salt water. Seams of hull caulked with special cotton payed and puttied. Outside of mahogany planking, finished in natural wood with spar varnish. Watertight bulkheads fore and aft which assist in floating the launch in case of accident. Decks and interior woodwork finished in selected Laguna mahogany. Steam bent quartered oak or mahogany coaming extending around cockpit."

Alvin Landon's launch was thirty-five feet long, with six-cylinder, sixty-horse power motor and a guaranteed speed of twenty-four miles an hour. The motor was placed under the forward deck, where it was fully protected by a hinged metal deck. To become somewhat technical again let me proceed:

All the valves were placed on the same side, the camshaft (operating the valves) as well as the pump shaft being mounted on ball bearings. The crankcase was of tough aluminum alloy, and lubrication was well provided for, being kept at a constant level in the crankcase by a geared oil pump. A gear-driven pump circulated the necessary cooling water for the cylinders, which passed out through the copper exhaust pipe at the stern. Only one operating lever was employed and that was placed directly at the helmsman's left hand. The gasoline tank contained fifty gallons and was under the after deck with a pan below it for safety's sake, draining overboard. The propeller wheel and shaft were of bronze.

Alvin's motor boat, thus partially described, included the necessary deck hardware, "such as brass chocks and cleats, flag pole sockets and flag poles, ventilators to engine compartment, rubber matting for floor, cushions and upholstered backs for seats, three sailing lights, oars, rowlocks and sockets, compressed air whistle with tank, two pairs of cork fenders, bell, foghorn, boat hook and portable bilge pump, six life preservers (as required by the U. S. Government), a twenty-pound folding anchor and a hundred feet of strong manila rope."

We must not forget the glass wind-shield. Passengers and crew were always guarded against flying spray and sweep of wind and rain. Nothing that forethought could provide for the safety and comfort of all was forgotten.

Suppose young Captain Landon stepped on board the Deerfoot with the intention of starting out on a cruise. He would first turn on the switch which controls the electric current for the jump spark, open the valve that allows the gasoline to flow from the tank into the carburettor, swing around the fly-wheel and then assume charge of the lever and steering gear. But lo! the engine refuses to respond. There is no motion. What is the cause?

There may be a dozen of them. In the first place, the battery may be worn out; there may be a lack of compression due to leaky valves; perhaps, after all, he forgot to place the switch key in position; the spark plugs may be fouled or cracked, the gasoline shut off, the gas mixture imperfect, no gasoline in the tank, water in the cylinder caused by a leak from the water jacket, or water in the gasoline.

It may be that when the launch has covered a good many miles the engine suddenly stops. The cause may be faulty ignition, because of a disconnected wire or a loose terminal, exhaustion of the gasoline, or derangement of the magneto, or poor carburettor adjustment.

But I have said enough to give you an idea of what the expert handler of a motor boat must understand. It may seem almost a hopeless task, but, as I stated at the beginning of this chapter, patience and application will enable you to overcome all difficulties and make the handling of the craft an unalloyed pleasure.

CHAPTER VI. Captain and Crew

When the elder Landon received a report from the principal of the military school on the Hudson to the effect that Alvin led all his classmates in their studies and had not once been brought under discipline, he was glad to fulfil the promise made months before, and bought him a handsome motor launch, the selection of which was left to the youth himself. The craft was shipped to Portland, Maine, there set afloat in the capacious bay and sped northeastward for forty miles or so, to the bungalow which the banker had erected a year before on Southport Island. The retreat was to be used by him and his family as a restful refuge from the feverish work which kept him in New York most of the year, with occasional flying trips to the great cities in the West or as far as the Pacific coast.

One condition the parent insisted upon: Alvin was not to run the launch alone until an expert pronounced him qualified to do so. Thus it was that when the boat headed up Casco Bay, Captain Abe Daboll, from the factory, was aboard and directed things. He had overseen the construction of the launch and knew all about it from stem to stern. He was there under engagement to deliver it to the bungalow, or rather as near as he could approach the building, and to remain and instruct Alvin in every point necessary for him to know.

Several facts joined to make the youth an apt pupil. He was naturally bright and was intensely interested in all that related to motor boats. While awaiting the completion of his launch, he read and studied many catalogues, circulars and books relating to such craft, and rode in a number. He asked questions and studied the working of the machinery and handling of the launch until his instructor looked at him in wonderment.

"I never saw your equal," he said admiringly; "by and by you will be answering my questions and telling me how to run things."

The smiling youth knew this was exaggeration, for something new seemed to be turning up continually, and there were turns where he thought he knew the way, only to find when put to the test that he was totally ignorant. But as I said, he learned fast and after a week's stay at the home of Mr. Landon, during every day of which—excepting Sunday—the two went on a cruise with Alvin at the helm, the man said that nothing more remained for him to show his pupil. This remark followed a stormy day when the launch went far south beyond Damariscove Island and was caught in a rough sea.

"It was the real test," said the expert to the banker. "I never raised my hand or made a suggestion when we were plunging through the big seas, for neither was necessary. You needn't be afraid to trust yourself with him anywhere and in any weather."

Now that I am through with my rather lengthy, but perhaps necessary introduction, let us proceed with the story I have set out to tell.

On the morning following the battle of Alvin with his assailants, and his pleasing meeting with Mike Murphy, the youth called at the home of the Irish lad, carrying in his hand a yachting cap in addition to the one he wore on his own head. Across the front were the gilt letters Deerfoot.

"I bought an extra one when I had my suit made," he explained, "and it looks to me as if it will fit you. A straw hat isn't handy to wear when sailing, even though you may loop the string around its band into your button hole. If the season was not so far along, I should order a yachting suit for you, Mike. You know a mate ought to be in uniform. But we shall have to wait till next summer."

The grinning lad gingerly took the white cap in hand, turned it about and then pulled it over his crown. He was in front of his own home, and his father as he smoked his pipe looked on, the mother being out of sight within the house. The headgear fitted perfectly.

"It's a pity to waste such fine wear on the hid of so ugly looking a spalpeen," remarked the father; "in trooth it ill becomes him."

"How can ye have the heart to blame me, dad, that I was born wid such a close resimblance to yersilf that if we was the same age mither couldn't till us apart?"

The parent was about to reply to this personal remark, but ignored his offspring and spoke to Alvin.

"Ye have a foine day for a sail, Captain."

"It is perfect."

"And Chister Haynes goes wid yes?"

"We are partners all the way through and he's expecting me."

"The sicond mate hasn't the honor of an acquaintance with the first mate, but it won't take us long to larn aich ither's ways," said Mike, bubbling over with high spirits and the promise of a day of rare enjoyment. "The mate hasn't the right to make suggistions to the captain, but if he had he would venture to obsarve that he is wasting vallyble time talking wid a gentleman who can't tell a gasoline launch from a lobster pot———"

"Be the same token he can till a lobster when he sees him," exclaimed the parent in pretended wrath, making a dive for his son, who eluded him by darting into the highway. Alvin waved a good-by to Pat and the youths hurried away, anxious to be out on the water.

While following the road toward the home of Chester Haynes, Mike took off his cap and admiringly surveyed it. He noted the patent leather visor, the gilt buttons to which the chin strap was attached, and then spelled out the name on the front.

"I 'spose that is what your boat is called, Captain?" he remarked inquiringly.

43

"Yes; you know it's the fashion for sailors on a man-of-war thus to show the name of the ship to which they belong."

"But why didn't the sign painter git the word roight?"

"What do you mean, Mike? Isn't that the correct way to spell 'Deerfoot'?"

"I 'spose the first part might go, as me uncle obsarved whin the front of his shanty fell down, but the rear is wrong."

"You mean 'foot.' What is wrong about it?"

"The same should be 'fut': that's the way we spell it in Ireland."

"We have a different method here," gravely remarked Alvin.

"And if I may ask, Captain, where did you git the name from?"

"Have you ever read about Deerfoot the Shawanoe? He was such a wonderful young Indian that I guess he never lived. But Chester and I became fond of him, and when Chester thought it would be a good idea to name the boat for him I was glad to do so."

"Deerfut the Shenanigan," repeated Mike. "Where can I maat the gintleman?"

"Oh, he's been dead these many years,—long before you or I was born."

"Wurrah, wurrah, what a pity!" and Mike sighed as if from regret. "Are you sure that isn't him that's coming up the road?"

A youth of about the age of Alvin, but of lighter build, and dressed like him in yachting costume, came into sight around a slight bend in the highway.

"That's Chester; he's so anxious to take advantage of this beautiful day that he has come to meet us, though he might have used the boat for part of the way since he is well able to handle it."

A few minutes later Chester and Mike were introduced. No one could help being pleased with the good-natured Irish youth, and the two warmly shook hands.

"Mike did me such a fine service last night that I must tell you about it," remarked Alvin as the three walked southward.

"Arrah, now, ye make me blush," protested Mike, "as I said whin they crowned me Queen of May in the owld counthry."

Alvin, however, related the whole story and you may be sure it lost none in the narration. Mike insisted that the Captain had done a great deal more than he to bring about a glorious victory.

"I believe every word Alvin has told me," was the comment of Chester; "and I am proud to have you with us as a friend."

"Such being the case," added Alvin, "I have as a slight token of my appreciation, made Mike my first mate, with you as second, and all three as the crew of theDeerfoot."

"There couldn't be a finer appointment," assented Chester. "I suppose, Mate Murphy, you know all about sailing a boat?"

"I larned the trade in the owld counthry, by sailing me mither's old shoe in a tub of water; I 'spose the same is all that is nicessary."

"That is sufficient, but," and the manner of Chester was grave, "you two make light of what is a pretty serious matter. That attack upon you was a crime that ought to be punished."

"I'm thinking it has been," said Mike; "I belave the rapscallions are of the same mind."

"No doubt they meant to rob you."

"And would have succeeded but for Mike. We never saw them before, have no idea who they are, or how they came to be in this part of Maine, nor where they have gone."

"Would you know either if you met him by day?"

"I am not sure, though the moonlight gave me a pretty fair view. It wasn't a time for a calm inspection."

"I'm sure I would know the chap that I had the run in wid," said Mike.

"How?"

"By his black eye and smashed nose."

"They might help. They were dressed well, but I can't understand what caused them to visit Southport and to lie in wait for me."

"Have there been any burglaries or robberies in the neighborhood?"

"None, so far as I have heard. You know there have been a number of post office robberies among the towns to the north, but it can't be that those two fellows have had anything to do with them."

"Probably not, and yet it is not impossible. I often wonder why there are not more crimes of that kind at the seaside and mountain resorts, where there are so many opportunities offered. The couple you ran against may belong to some gang who have decided to change their field of operations."

"If so we shall soon hear of them again."

"Arrah, now, if we could only maat them agin!" sighed the wistful Mike. "It would make me young once more."

CHAPTER VII. One August Day

"Well, here we are!"

It was Captain Alvin Landon who uttered the exclamation as the three came to a halt on the shore at the point nearest the moorings of the gasoline launch Deerfoot, left there the night before.

She made a pretty picture, with her graceful lines, shining varnish, polished brass work and cleanliness everywhere. The steersman in the cockpit was guarded by a wind-shield of thick glass. At the stern floated a flag displaying an anchor surrounded by a circle of stars with the stripes as shown in our national emblem. At the bow flew a burgee or small swallow-tailed flag of blue upon which was the word Deerfoot in gold. The bunting was always taken in when the boat lay up for the night, but in daytime and in clear weather it was displayed on the launch.

Not only could one sleep with some comfort on such a craft by using the convertible seats, but food could be prepared on an oil stove. In cruising, however, among the numerous islands and bays, it was so easy to go ashore for an excellent meal that Captain Landon followed the rule.

The water was so deep close to land that the three easily sprang aboard, the Captain being last in order to cast off the line that held the boat in place. It was the first time that Mike Murphy had ever placed foot on a craft of that nature. While Chester hustled about, Alvin quickly joining him, he gaped around in silent amazement. He felt that in his ignorance of everything the best course for him was to do nothing without the advice of his young friends. He sank down gingerly on one of the seats and watched them.

He saw the Captain thrust the switch plug into place, though with no idea of what he meant by doing so, while Chester took a peep into the gasoline tank in the stern. Then Alvin opened the hinged deck which covered the big six cylinder motor, climbed forward to the fly-wheel, and swung it back and forth until it circled over. Instantly there followed a smooth whirr, and he closed the forward deck over the motor and took his seat behind the wind-shield where he grasped the wheel which, as on an automobile, controlled the steering gear. The control lever, as has been stated, was on his left. Alvin pushed this forward until the clutch took hold, and with a churning of the screw at the stern the boat moved ahead and quickly attained a good degree of speed. The wind was so slight that the surface of the water was scarcely rippled, and no motion could be felt except the vibration of the powerful engine.

The bow and stern lines having been neatly coiled down and everything being adjusted, with Captain Alvin seated and loosely grasping the steering wheel, the two mates took their places behind him, prepared to enjoy the outing to the full. Youth, high health, with every surrounding circumstance favorable—what can bring more happiness to a human being? They come to us only once and let us make the most of them.

"Is it permitted to spake to the man at the wheel?" called Mike to the Captain, who, looking over his shoulder, nodded his head.

"So long as you speak good sense."

"Which the same is what I does always; why couldn't ye take a run over to Ireland this morning, now that ye are headed that way?"

"It's worth thinking about, but we shall have to wait till another time. Better become acquainted with a part of the Maine coast first."

The launch was speeding to the northeast in the direction of Squirrel Island, which has long been one of the most popular of summer resorts. This beautiful spot is not quite a mile long and has a varied scenery that surprises everyone who visits the place. The deep water around the wharf is as clear as crystal, so that at high tide one can look down and see clearly the rocky bottom twenty feet below. The coast abounds with prodigious rocks tumbled together by some stupendous convulsion of nature and against which the waves dash with amazing power during a storm, and throw the spray high in air and far inland. There are shady woods of balsam and fir where one may stroll in the cool twilight over the velvet carpet, meandering along the bewitching "Lover's Walk," with which nearly every section is provided, or threading his way through the dense bushes which brush him lovingly as he follows the faintly marked paths. Overhead, when the crow sentinels catch sight of him, they caw their warnings to their comrades. There are shadowy glens, gaping fissures, whose corresponding faces show that at some remote age they were split apart by a terrific upheaval, a gray barn with its threshing machine and air of quiet country life, rows of neat cottages, a little white wooden church, perched like a rooster gathering himself and about to crow and flap his wings, the Casino, smooth, grassy slopes, and at the northern end of the island, the roomy Squirrel Inn, crowded with visitors attracted by the cool and bracing air, from the opening to the close of summer.

Our young friends had no intention of calling there, but, circling to the westward of the island, headed for Boothbay Harbor nestling three miles to the northward. A number of girls loitering on the broad porch of the hotel and a group playing tennis waved their handkerchiefs; the young Captain answered with a tooting of his whistle, and Mike Murphy rising to his feet swung his cap over his head.

To the right stretched Linekin Bay, to the head of Linekin Neck, beyond which courses the Damariscotta River, bristling with islets, picturesque and beautiful beyond compare. Captain Landon turned slightly to the left, still heading with unabated speed for Boothbay Harbor. He saw coming toward him a little steamer from whose bow the water spread in a foaming wake. It was the craft which makes regular trips between Boothbay Harbor and Squirrel Island through the summer season, stopping at other places when passengers wish it. One of these is Spruce Point, where little parties often go ashore over the rickety dock, and, striking into the shady woods, follow the winding path along the rocky coast known as the "Indian Trail," for more than two miles, when, after passing Mount Pisgah and crossing a long bridge, they find themselves in the town of which I have spoken.

As the two boats rapidly approached, passing within a short distance of each other, the head and shoulders of the captain of the Nellie G. showed in the pilot-house. He was a tall, handsome man with dark whiskers, who, when saluted by the Deerfoot, reached up and pulled the whistle cord of his own craft. Everyone knows Captain Williams of Bowdoinham and is glad to see him turn an honest penny each summer. His boat, one of the prettiest in those waters, had been built wholly by himself, and the name painted in big letters on the front of the wheelhouse is that of his wife.

To the left and almost touching Southport is Capitol Island, a little nearer, Burnt, and then Mouse, all as picturesque as they can be. The pathway arched with trees completely shades the sloping walk that leads to the hotel on Mouse Island. A government light on Burnt Island throws out its warning rays at momentary intervals through the night. When fog settles down, the light gives place to a tolling bell.

Entering the broad harbor, our friends saw a score or more of vessels grouped around at anchor, or moored at the wharves. There was a magnificent yacht, the property of a multimillionaire of national reputation; another luxurious craft, the representative of a Boston club, a five-masted schooner, veteran ships, two of which had voyaged from the other side of the world, a decayed and rotting hull near the long bridge, where it tipped a little to one side in the mud, and was wholly under water when the tide was in, as it had been for years. An excursion steamer from Bath was just arriving, while others were taking on passengers for some of the towns not far off.

Alvin, having slowed down by lessening the amount of gas admitted to the cylinders with the throttle lever on the wheel, rounded to at one of the floats, where a man who had noted his approach caught the loop of rope tossed to him and slipped it over the mooring pile set in place for that purpose. The steersman pulled the control lever back to the vertical position, releasing the propeller shaft from connection with the motor. A further pull backward threw in the reverse gear, and the launch came to rest beside the float and the lever was returned to the vertical position.

"I'll look after it while you are gone," he said and Alvin nodded. Captain and crew then attended to stopping the motor by turning the switch to the "off" position, putting out fenders to avoid scratching, making bow and stern lines fast to deck cleats and putting everything in shipshape order.

The three then climbed the steps to the upper level, passed the storehouses and ascended the moderate hill to the principal street of the well-known town of Boothbay Harbor. There was little that was noteworthy in the rather long avenue, lined with the usual stores, a bank and amusement hall and a number of pretty residences, and I should make no reference to it except for an incident that befell the visitors.

Having gone to the end of the street, that is, until the eastern terminal gave way to the open country, they turned about to retrace their steps to the boat, for it was much more pleasant to be skimming over the water. The temperature at Boothbay Harbor is generally five or ten degrees higher than at Squirrel Island.

The three sauntered along, pausing now and then to look into the store windows, admiring the displays of Indian trinkets offered for sale, and approached the corner where they were to turn down the hill to the wharf. At that moment they saw a man of dark complexion, with a big mustache, and accompanied by a large lad, both in yachting costume, come out of Hodgdon's store, which is devoted to the sale of hats, caps, boots, shoes, clothing and other necessities. The two took the opposite course, following the main street in the direction of the ball grounds.

Neither Alvin nor Chester did more than glance at the couple, for there was nothing unusual in their appearance, but Mike started.

"Did ye obsarve thim?" he asked, lowering his voice.

"Yes; but there are plenty others on the street that are as interesting."

"Come wid me," whispered Mike, "say nothing."

He whisked into the store, his wondering companions at his heels. They left the situation to him.

"Will ye oblige me by saying whither the two that has just passed out bought anything of ye?" asked Mike of the rotund, smiling clerk, who, hesitating a moment, answered:

"The younger one bought a yachting cap, or rather traded one for his old straw hat, for which I allowed him a nickel, which is all it's worth and more too, I'm beginning to think."

He held up the dilapidated headgear which he caught up from under the counter.

"Do ye recognize the same?" asked Mike, in a whisper of Alvin.

"Can it be possible!" exclaimed the young Captain.

"It's the identycal hat I wore last night whin we had our ilegant shindy!"

CHAPTER VIII. A Passing Glimpse

Mike Murphy, even in the flurry of the moment, could not forget his innate courtesy. He handed back the old hat to the puzzled clerk and bowed.

"I thank ye very much for yer kindness, and now, lads, come wid me."

He hurried out of the door, the two following closely.

"What do you mean to do?" asked Alvin.

"Folly the chap and finish the shindy I started wid him," replied the Irish lad, staring in the direction taken by the couple. "Ye can luk on and kaap back the man, so that I'll git fair play wid the ither."

"You are not on the Southport road, Mike," warned Alvin, "and you will be arrested before you can land a blow and probably locked up."

"It'll be worth it," replied the other, scenting the battle like a war horse. "Bad luck to it! Where is the spalpeen?"

The three were looking keenly up the street, but, brief as was the interval, the couple had vanished.

There are a number of lesser streets which lead inland at right angles to the main avenue of Boothbay

Harbor, and almost as many that are mere alleys on the other side, through which one may pass to the different wharves. It will be seen, therefore, that there was nothing strange in the disappearance of the strangers in whom our friends were so much interested.

"They can't have gone fur," exclaimed the impatient Mike, hesitating for the moment as to what was best to do, and feeling the value of every passing minute and fearing lest the opportunity be lost.

"They must have come in a boat," suggested Chester, "and have turned down one of the by-streets to the water. But what is the purpose of chasing them?"

"So we may catch 'em," was the reply of Mike, who feeling there was a possibility that they might have turned the other way, addressed Chester:

"Cross to the ither side of the main street and hurry by the corners, looking up aich as ye do so; if they've turned that way, they're still in sight."

There was sense in the plan. Chester ran across the avenue and walked rapidly, glancing up each opening as he came to it. He meant merely to keep the couple in sight until he could learn something more of them. At the same time he was wise enough to avoid drawing attention to himself. He passed well beyond the hotel without catching sight of the man and boy and finally stopped, convinced that it was useless to go farther.

Alvin Landon was of the same mind with him. As matters stood, nothing was to be gained by accusing the youth of assault and attempted robbery, for no proof could be brought forward. Moreover, his companion at that time was absent, the man now with him having been seen for the first time by Alvin and Mike a few minutes before.

"It will be well to learn something of the two," the Captain thought to himself, "but it will be a mistake to make them suspect us, as they are sure to do if they find we are dogging them. As for Mike pitching in and starting another fight, it will be the height of folly. I won't allow it."

The two were walking side by side and going so fast that several persons looked curiously at them.

"Take it easy," advised Alvin.

"The same is what I'll do whin I comes up wid the spalpeen, that stole me hat where I'd flung it in the road."

"Keep cool and if you get sight of them, don't go nearer, but watch———"

"There they be now!" exclaimed Mike at the first glance down one of the alleys on their left, and, before Alvin could check him, he dashed off at his best speed. His progress might have been satisfactory, but when half way down the hill someone pushed the front of a wheelbarrow through a door and across the way. Its appearance was so unexpected and close that Mike could not check himself nor had he time in which to gather for the leap that would clear it. He struck the obstacle fairly and went over, landing on his hands and knees, while the barrow in turn toppled upon him. The urchin who had caused the mischief turned and fled in a panic, before the indignant Mike could chastise him.

Alvin rested his hand against the nearest building and laughed until he could hardly save himself from falling. Resuming his uncertain walk he called:

"Are you hurt, Mike?"

"Oh, no," replied the lad, rubbing his shins and screwing up his face with the smart of the bumps he had received; "as me second cousin said whin he fell from the steeple, I've only broke both legs, one arm and bent me head out of shape—nothin' worth the mintion. I come nigh forgettin' my arrant."

And unmindful of the hurts, which were trifling, he dashed down the slope, arriving a minute later at the wharf, where a dozen men and several boys were loading or unloading craft, or boarding or coming ashore from some boat. Although Mike would not admit it, he had fixed his suspicion upon a man who when he turned his face proved to be fully fifty years old, while his companion was a lusty colored youth. He glanced here and there and at all the craft in sight. Possibly his eyes rested upon the right one, but he saw neither of the persons whom he sought, and faced about as Alvin joined him.

"They have give us the slip—bad cess to 'em, for I make nothing of the spalpeens among them in sight."

The two scanned all the craft that suggested ownership by the strangers, but it was in vain. Then they made their way along the wharves to where they had left theDeerfoot. Chester was awaiting them and shook his head as they approached. Alvin paid the man who had looked after the boat in his absence, and after casting off and starting the motor, the three headed for Christmas Cove, where the Captain said they would have dinner, though they would arrive before the regular hour for that meal. Progress was so easy that conversation kept up with the Captain while he held the steering wheel.

"I suspect from what we saw awhile ago that the fellows whom Mike and I met last night belong to a gang. One of them is a man and there may be others."

"It is lucky the younger did not recognize either of you," said Chester. "Do you think he would do so if you met face to face?"

"There is no reason why he should not, for Mike identified him with only a passing glance. You must remember that the sky was clear and the moon bright."

"It's mesilf that belaves we imprissed ourselves upon their memory," said Mike so gravely that the others knew he meant the words as a jest. Alvin was silent for a moment and then turned his head, for the wheel required little attention.

"Mike, you acknowledge me as Captain and that my mate must obey orders?"

The remark was a question. The youth rose promptly to his feet and touched his forefinger to the front of his cap.

"I await yer orders, Captain."

"If we meet that fellow whose name we believe to be 'Noxon' you must not show that you have any suspicion of his identity, nor must you make any move against him without first consulting me."

Mike looked at the second mate.

"Isn't that enough to timpt one to mootiny? I obsarve that Mr. Noxon's right eye was of a bootiful black and blue color and the ither should be painted to match the same. It was him that was the thaif who stole me hat."

"Didn't you take his cap?"

"It was a fair prize of war—there's a moighty difference, as the lawyer said whin he larned it was the ither man's ox that was gored. But as I flung my tile away and he come back to git his own, I sha'n't lay it up agin him."

As the Deerfoot sped northeast again, the sharp cutwater splitting the wavelets to the tune of the big motor's humming, and following the main line of the Maine coast, the boys saw the small, low-lying Ram Island and its light on their right, with Linekin Neck on the left, and Inner Heron Island showing in front. Gliding between this and the ledges known as the

Thread of Life, they speedily rounded to at the wharf at Christmas Cove. As elsewhere, there were yachts, sailboats and various kinds of craft at anchor or secured to the floats. To one of the latter the three friends made the launch fast and passed over the pier and by the hall where entertainments and religious services are held. The water so far north as Maine is as a rule too cold for popular bathing. At Christmas Cove this difficulty is overcome by a goodly sized pool into which the salt water is admitted at high tide, when the gates are closed and it is held until the time comes for changing it.

The opportunity was too good to be lost, and the youngsters each rented a suit and a bath house, from which they emerged and plunged delightedly into the pool. It will be remembered that Mike Murphy could not swim a stroke, but the pond is prepared for such persons, and all he had to do was to keep away from the corner near the gates, which is the only place where the water is beyond one's depth. Alvin and Chester were fine swimmers and dived and frolicked until they were sated. They tried to teach the rudiments of swimming to their comrade, but he made no progress and they had to give over the attempt for the time.

It was but a short climb to the Hollywood Inn, where the genial Landlord Thorpe gave them welcome and they wrote their names in the ledger. Then they walked out on the rear porch to admire the romantic scenery, while awaiting the dinner hour. On one side was the placid Cove, making up from the Damariscotta River and dotted with pleasure craft; on the other, John's Bay and the broad Atlantic. Pointing toward the historical Pemaquid Point, on the opposite side of the Bay, Alvin said to his companions:

"All looks calm and peaceful now, but how different it was on that September day in 1813!"

They turned inquiringly toward him.

"Right off yonder the American brig Enterprise of fourteen guns, commanded by Captain Burrows, fought the British Boxer, also of fourteen guns. It was a desperate battle in which both captains were killed and the British vessel captured. The prize was taken into Portland harbor, and the two commanders lie buried side by side in the city."

CHAPTER IX. No Man's Land

Lying a short distance off the Maine coast is an island which belongs to nobody and is therefore referred to as No Man's Land. If you look for it on the map you will find it marked as Muscongus. It is also known as Loud's Island, in honor of the first settler. The strange state of affairs came about in this way:

The Lincolnshire or Muscongus Patent, granted in 1630 by the Council of Plymouth to Beauchamp and Leverett, included the land from the seaboard, between the Muscongus and Penobscot rivers, for a certain distance inland, but made no mention of the island on the south. The grant passed to General Samuel Waldo, and was the origin of most of the land titles in that section of Maine.

One of the most honored names in colonial England is that of Samoset, the Wampanoag Indian, who met the first Plymouth settlers with the English greeting, "Welcome, Englishmen!" He had picked up a few words from the fishermen who made their headquarters at Monhegan, an island ten miles farther out to sea. Samoset was accustomed to spend his summers on Muscongus. If you dig in the sand on the island you will be pretty sure to find relics of the aboriginal occupation of the place.

Captain Loud commanded a privateer in the service of George III, and one day lost his temper in a dispute over some prize money. The quarrel waxed so hot that he declared in his rage he would never lift his hand again

65

in the service of the king, even to save the monarch's head. Such lese majesté was sure to bring serious consequences to the peppery old salt, so he hurriedly sailed for Boston on his brig. While coasting the province of Maine, he came upon Muscongus, and was so charmed that he spent the remainder of his life there. In some way that no one can explain, the United States surveyors overlooked this island, three miles in length and a mile broad, and the mistake has never been corrected. Muscongus therefore remains no man's land.

It is well wooded and watered and has a picturesque shore, with rocky coves, white sandy beaches, and an attractive appearance from every direction. No steamer ever stops there, and it is rather ticklish business to pick your way over the crags to the dilapidated landing and so on to the firm land beyond.

The unique condition of Muscongus causes some queer things. For a long time, the people, who now number a hundred and twenty-five, paid taxes to the township of Bristol on the mainland two miles away. Every year the tax collector sailed or rowed over to Muscongus and marked in chalk on each door the amount of taxes due from that family. He gave his receipt for payment of the same by rubbing out the chalked figures.

This was a pleasing but one-sided arrangement. Bristol gained the sole advantage and by and by the Muscongus folks awoke to the fact. Then they refused to pay any taxes unless the collector showed legal authority for his assessment. The chalk marks were rubbed off the doors and after some spirited scenes the collector withdrew, since, as has been shown, he had no legal means of enforcing his demands. Since then Muscongus has been the only community in New England which is not taxed, except so far as it chooses to impose the burden upon itself.

Among the islanders every man was a Democrat with a single exception. At the Congressional election on the mainland the Republican candidate was unpopular, but the vote of Muscongus was cast for and elected him. The canvassers, however, threw out the vote because of the refusal to pay taxes. This was just before the Civil War, and in the words of the chronicler of Muscongus: "That was the end of all things here in connection with the mainland."

You need not be reminded that as the great war went on the government was forced to resort to drafting to obtain the soldiers it needed. Muscongus was included in the Bristol district, but the inhabitants warned the authorities that any attempt to enforce the draft would cause bloodshed. Some of them, however, were alarmed at the thought of fighting the national government. At a mass meeting the community voted to donate nine hundred dollars toward the expense of the war, and a number paid three hundred dollars apiece for substitutes, though none volunteered. These contributions meant many sacrifices to the poor fisher folk.

A man living on Muscongus had once served in the regular army, and a certain major at Bristol determined to secure him for Uncle Sam. The officer was taken over to the island in a small sailboat, and made his way to the home of the veteran he wanted. He was absent, but his wife was in the kitchen peeling potatoes. A few minutes later the major's companions awaiting him at the shore saw him dash through the door and run at his highest speed for the boat. A few paces behind him, holding the pan of potatoes against her side with one hand, and snatching them out with the other, she bombarded the terrified fugitive. She could throw, too, with the force and accuracy of a short stop of the professional league, and every missile landed. She kept up the bombardment all the way to the waterside, by which time her ammunition was used up. When the battered major stepped ashore at Bristol he exclaimed:

"Thunderation! If I had a regiment of women like her I'd capture Richmond in three days!"

The foregoing facts Captain Alvin Landon related to Chester Haynes and Mike Murphy one sunshiny forenoon as the Deerfoot swept past the numerous islands between Cape Newagen and Pemaquid Point, and rounded to at the rickety landing on the southern side of Muscongus. The boys stepped out upon the rocks, leaping and climbing to the wabbling support over which they picked their way to the solid earth. A few rods distant a goodly sized sailboat was moored, the passengers having already gone up the sloping bank and inland. Hardly a fair summer day goes by without bringing visitors to one of the most interesting spots on the coast of Maine.

Since the excursion was likely to take most of the afternoon, our young friends brought their lunch with them. At the crest of the slope, they sat down on the grass under a group of trees, and with keen appetites ate the last morsel of their meal. Then followed a stroll, with ears and eyes open. They found the islanders courteous, hospitable and ready to answer all questions. One of the first interesting facts learned by the youthful callers was that nearly all the people were blue-eyed, and the men straight, tall, rugged and with a physique superior to that of their neighbors on the mainland. Several descendants of the Loud and other pioneers were met, one or two of whom were approaching the century mark. Contentment was everywhere, and all were proud of their independent lives with not the slightest wish to change it. Some of the men seek their wives outside of the little model republic, and more than one husband has been drawn to the island by the attraction of a pair of violet eyes and the sweet disposition of a coy maiden. It has been charged that there is a mental and physical deterioration because of intermarriages between relatives, but nothing of the kind seems to have occurred.

Muscongus knows little, except by hearsay, of crime and pauperism. All the doors are left unlocked at night, and a drunken person is never seen. Should any fall in need of charity it is given cheerfully. Years ago there was an aged couple whose five sons were lost at sea, and who were unable to provide for themselves. They were supported in comfort in their own home as long as they lived.

Of course there has to be some form of government. It is of the simplest nature. All general meetings are held in the little schoolhouse, the only public building on the island. The presiding officer is chosen by acclamation, and is always the school agent and superintendent of business of the community. An open discussion follows of the measures needed for the public welfare, and whatever rules are adopted are obeyed without protest.

In former years the porgy industry was the chief support. But that declined and was succeeded by lobster and mackerel fishing, which does not pay so well. Every family owns a little farm, the soil is good, and all live in modest comfort. The neat, tidy houses nestling among the firs are surrounded by fruit trees trim and productive. The small library in the schoolhouse is free to all.

As to religious services, a prayer meeting is held every Sunday evening in the schoolhouse and Sunday School in the afternoon, but there is no resident minister. Occasionally the clergyman at Friendship, near Bristol, comes over to preach, and the faithful coast missionary who works among remote islanders and lighthouse keepers brings reading matter and ministers to the spiritual wants of the people. Among the islanders are Free Masons, Odd Fellows, Knights of Pythias and Red Men, who conduct the funeral services.

"It calls to mind the ould counthry," said Mike Murphy, when the Deerfoot had started homeward.

"How?" asked Chester at his side.

"It's so different; think if ye can of any part of Ireland living for a waak, lit alone months and years, widout a shindy."

"There are few sections in our own country of which that can be said."

"It taxes me mind to thry to draw the painful picter; let us think of something else."

Since the weather was favorable, Captain Landon made a circuit farther south, leaving the small White Islands on his left, the Hypocrites on his right, and so on into the broad bay, whose western boundary is Southport.

"I say, Captain," suddenly called Mike.

"What is it?" asked Landon, looking partly round.

"If ye have no objiction I should like to take a thrick at the wheel."

"All right; come over here."

In a twinkling the two had changed places. As Mike assumed his duty, he added:

"I've been obsarving ye so close that I belave I can run the battleship as well as yersilf. I have noted that whin ye wish to turn to the right, ye move the wheel around that way, sarving it according whin ye wish to head t'other way. 'Spose now ye find it nicessary to go backward?"

"Pull over the reversing lever; the wheel has nothing to do with that."

"I'll remember the same. Hullo!" added Mike in some excitement. "I obsarve a ship ahead; do ye think it's a pirate?"

His companions laughed and Alvin answered:

"That is the steamer Enterprise, which runs from Portland to East Boothbay and back on alternate days, calling at different points."

"I mustn't run her down," said Mike, swinging over the wheel so as to pass her bow; "she's right in our path."

"Don't change your course; she has plenty of time to get out of your way."

"Begorrah! Do ye maan to say she is moving?"

His companions scrutinized the lumbering craft for a minute as if in doubt. It was Chester who said:

"I think she is."

"Better make sure," remarked Mike heading the launch to the south, thus contributing his part to a joke which has been fashionable for years in that section of the Union over the sluggishness of the freight and passenger steamer named.

CHAPTER X. The Lure of Gold

It was borne in upon Gideon Landon when he rounded the half century mark that he must let up in his intense application to his vast moneyed interests or break down. He hated to think of stopping, even for a brief season, but nature gave her unerring warning and the specialist whom he consulted spoke tersely and to the point:

"Take a vacation every year or die."

The capitalist recalled the habit of Bismarck, the great German Chancellor, who when worn out by the crushing cares of office hied away to his cabin in the pine woods, and gave orders to the sentinels at the gate to shoot all visitors unless they came directly from the King. So Landon built him a palatial bungalow, as he called it, near the southern end of Southport Island. The logs, all with their bark on, were a foot in diameter. From the outside, the structure looked rough and rugged, and little more than a good imitation of the dwellings of the New England pioneers; but you had only to peep through the windows to note its splendid furnishings. The finest of oriental rugs covered the floor; chairs, tables and lounges were of the richest make, and the hundreds of choice books in their mahogany cases cost twice as many dollars. A modern machine furnished the acetylene light, the broad fireplace could take in a half cord of wood when the weather was too cool for comfort without it, and the beds on the upper floors were as soft and inviting as those in the banker's city residence. In short, everything that wealth could provide and for which there was a wish was at the service of the inmates. He offered to send a Chickering piano, but his wife did not think it worthwhile, as she had no daughter and neither she nor her husband played. Alvin had been taking lessons, for several years, but he objected to keeping up practice during vacation and his parents decided that his views were well founded.

"Here I shall loaf and rest for six weeks!" exclaimed the owner, when the chauffeur carried him, his wife and two servants from the town of Southport to the new home.

Alvin had gone thither the week before, and was looked after by Pat Murphy, the caretaker, and his wife, who had been long in the service of the banker.

One cause of Landon taking this step was the example of his old friend Franklin Haynes, who had only one child—Chester, with whom you have become acquainted. His enthusiastic accounts of the tonic effect of the air, confirmed by his own renewed vigor and tanned skin, decided the elder in his course. The Haynes bungalow was smaller and more modest than Landon's, the two being separated by a half mile of woods and open country. This, however, was of no account, for the Landon auto skimmed over the interval in a few minutes and the interchange of visits went on day and night. The two families played bridge, dined, automobiled and cruised with each other, while the boys were inseparable.

This went on for a fortnight, when a break came. Landon and Haynes were interested in a large financial deal, in which the latter believed he was wronged. There was a sharp quarrel and the friendly relations between the two, including their wives, snapped apart. All bridge playing ceased, and the long summer hours became so deadly dull for Mrs. Landon that she gladly accepted the invitation of a friend, hurried to New York and sailed with her for England and the continent. Haynes spent his time mainly in fishing and reading, but kept away from the home of his rich neighbor, who was equally careful not to approach the other's residence.

Both men, however, were too sensible to let their quarrel affect their sons. Not the slightest shadow could come between those chums, who visited back and forth, just as they had always done, stopping over night wherever convenient, and as happy as two clean-minded, healthy youngsters ought to be. The Landon auto was at the disposal of the lads whenever they cared for it, but the youths had become interested in motor boating and gave little attention to the land vehicle.

The unpleasant break to which I have referred occurred about a fortnight before my introduction of the two lads to you. Landon never had any liking for athletics or sport. Every favorable morning his chauffeur took him to the little cluster of houses called Southport, at the head of the island, where he got his letters, New York newspapers and such supplies as happened to be needed at the house. This used up most of the first half of the day. After lunch he read, slept and loafed, never using the auto and caring nothing for the motor launch which was continually cruising over the water.

This went well enough for ten days or so, by which time the banker grew restless. Sleeping so much robbed him of rest at night. Classic works lost their charm and the "best sellers" bored him. He yawned, strolled about his place, and pitied every man who was doomed to spend his life in the Pine Tree State. True, he was gaining weight and his appetite became keen, but he smoked too much and was discontented. The lure of Wall Street was drawing him more powerfully every day. He longed to plunge into the excitement with his old time zest, and to enjoy the thrill that came when success ended a financial battle.

He was lolling in his hammock at the front of the bungalow one afternoon, trying to read and to smoke one of his heavy black cigars, and succeeding in neither task, when Davis Dunning, his chauffeur, glummer than usual because there was no excuse for his taking any more joy rides, halted the machine at the side of the roadway. Throwing out the clutch, he hurried up the walk and handed his employer a telegram that had been 'phoned over from Boothbay Harbor to Southport, where the chauffeur found it awaiting him when he made his daily run thither, this time unaccompanied by his employer.

No message could have been more welcome. It told the banker that the recent stir in steel and other stocks made it necessary for him to return to New York as soon as possible and to stay "a few days." He was alert on the instant. If he could reach Portland that evening he would board the express and be in New York the next morning.

"It must be done!" he exclaimed, aware that there was no necessity for such haste. Consultation with Dunning, however, convinced him that the course for an automobile was too roundabout and there was too much ferrying to make the hurried journey feasible. He decided to go to Bath by steamer, and then by rail on the morrow, easily reaching Portland in time for the ride by night to the metropolis.

This gave him opportunity to explain matters to Alvin, who was told to remain at Southport until the time came for him to re-enter school. The son was sorry to lose the company of his father, whose affection he returned, but it is not in boy nature to mourn for one from whom he did not expect to be parted long. The only thing in creation in which he felt pleasure and interest just then was in sailing his motor boat.

At the time of leaving Southport, Mr. Landon expected to return in the course of a week and said so to his son, but the call of business was stronger than that of the fine woods and salt water of Maine. He easily found the necessity for staying in New York until the time remaining for his vacation was so brief that he wrote Alvin it was not worthwhile to rejoin him.

So it came about that his son remained in the big bungalow, looked after by two servants, not to mention Pat Murphy the caretaker and his wife. Chester Haynes stayed with his parents in their modest home a mile to the southward, while the irrepressible Mike was at both homes more than his own. He had become as fond of boating as his two friends and set out to learn all about the craft. It did not take him long to become a good steersman and by and by he could start and stop the Deerfoot, though he shrank from attempting to bring her beside a wharf or float. In threading through the shipping at the different harbors, either Alvin or

Chester took the wheel, one boy being almost equal in expertness to the other, both in handling the launch and taking care of the machinery.

There seemed no end to the romantic excursions that tempted the young navigators forth. Sometimes they fished, but preferred to glide through the smooth inland waters, where every scene was new and seemingly more romantic than the others. They landed at Pemaquid Beach and listened to the story of the old fort as told by the local historian, who proved that the date was correct which is painted on the stone wall and says a settlement was made there before the one at Jamestown. They passed up the short wide inlet known as John's River, and turning round cut across to the Damariscotta, which they ascended to Newcastle, with picturesque scenery all the way.

The boys were somewhat late in starting one morning and the sky was threatening, but with the folding top as a protection if needed, and the opportunity to halt when and wherever they choose, the agreement was unanimous that they should go up the Sheepscot to Wiscasset, eat dinner there and return at their leisure.

"It is well worth the trip," said Alvin, whose eyes sparkled with the memory of the passage which he had made more than once. Chester was equally enthusiastic.

"I'm riddy to sarve as a sacrifice," replied Mike, "as me friend Terry McGarrity remarked whin he entered the strife that was to prove which could ate the most mince pie inside of half an hour."

CHAPTER XI. A Missing Motor Boat

Swinging into the broad expanse of Sheepscot Bay, the Deerfoot moved smoothly up the river which bears the same name. Captain Landon held her to the moderate speed of fifteen miles or so an hour. There was no call for haste and he was wise not to strain the engine unnecessarily. To increase the rate would be imitating the man who drives his automobile at the highest clip, when he has to concentrate his attention upon the machine, with no appreciation of the beauties of the country through which he is plunging, and continually threatened by fatal accidents.

Alvin held the wheel, while Chester and Mike, seated behind him, kept intelligent trace of their progress by means of the fine map of the United States Geological Survey. The first point identified was Lower Mark Island on the right and close to Southport, then came Cat Ledges, Jold, Cedarbrush, the Hendrick Light, on the same side, while across loomed the pretty station known as Five Islands, one of the regular stopping places of the steamers going north or south. Omitting the smaller places, the next point which interested our friends was the Isle of Springs, one of the best known summer resorts in Sheepscot River. The landing was crowded with passengers, waiting for the steamer Gardiner from Augusta, the capital of the State, and on its way to rush through the strait north of Southport to its destination, Ocean Point beyond Squirrel Island.

The peculiarity about this plucky little steamer is that no craft that ever plowed through those waters is so dependable. Again and again she has made the long trip and not been out a single minute at any of the numerous landings. She has been called the "Pony of the Kennebec," and nothing less than an explosion of her boiler or a collision with another craft would make her tardy anywhere.

"There are many persons along the river and on the islands who set their watches and clocks by the Gardiner," said Alvin, speaking over his shoulder.

He glanced at his watch.

"I don't know when she is due at the Isle of Springs, but as I figure it she ought to be in sight now."

"And, begorrah! There she comes!" exclaimed Mike, pointing to the left toward Goose Rock Passage, leading from Knubble Bay to Sheepscot. The foaming billows tumbled away from the prow, as the boat drove resistlessly forward, and the whistle sounded for the landing. Many a time when rounding Capitol Island to the northwest of Squirrel, with a storm raging, the spray and water have been flung clean over the pilot house and slid over the upper deck and streamed away off the stern.

Chester Haynes saluted with the whistle, but the captain of the Gardiner gave no heed. His eye was upon the landing toward which he was steaming. When the freight had been tumbled ashore and the waiting cargo taken aboard, the gang planks were drawn in, lines cast off, and though a dozen passengers might be pointing toward the pier, shouting and waving hats or umbrellas, all would be left.

The resinous pine trees formerly including firs, larches and true cedars so thick that no spaces showed between, grew all the way down the rocky hills to the water's edge. The river, without a ripple except such as was made by passing craft, was as crystalline as a mountain spring. Here and there a rude drawing was scratched in the face of the cliffs, the work of the Indians who lived in that part of Maine before the Pilgrims landed at Plymouth. It was one continuous dream which never loses its charm for those who make the trip, no matter how often.

The sky remained overcast, though no rain fell, when the Deerfoot drove through the Eddy, where the current narrows and is very swift and deep. A bridge connects the mainland with Davis Island. The launch sat so low that there was no call to the bridge tender to open the draw. As it shot under, the peaks of the flagstaffs showed a foot below the planking.

They were now approaching the pretty town of Wiscasset, from which came the faint thrill of a locomotive whistle, as notice that at that point a traveler could change from boats to cars. The launch was sweeping round a bend in the river when Mike pointed to the right with the question:

"Phwat's that?"

"It is the famous blockhouse, built in 1807 for the protection of Wiscasset, four miles away, but it was never used because the town was never in danger."

The interesting structure, which you may have seen when gliding past in a boat, is octagonal in form, with one window on each face of the lower story, except on the one containing a narrow door approached by a single step of wood. As was the fashion in building blockhouses, the second story overhangs the first and on each face of this upper story is a square window with a long loop-hole placed horizontally on either side. The flat roof is surmounted by a slender cupola, also octagonal, with a window occupying nearly all the space of each face. The whole building is covered with shingles and for a long time after its erection it was surrounded by an elaborate system of earthworks.

The Deerfoot slackened its speed as it came opposite. Mike Murphy showed special interest in the old faded building.

"It suggists the palace of me grandfather, the Duke De Sassy," said he. "If ye have no great objiction, Captain, I should be glad of a closer look at it."

Since the day was at their disposal, the youthful captain was quite willing to halt and inspect the historic structure. He turned the bow toward the bank, and stopped in deep water a few feet from land. Mike cleared the intervening distance in an easy jump, taking the end of the bow line which he made fast to a convenient tree. Chester at the same time had cast out the anchor from the stern and made fast the cable to a cleat on the after or stern deck. The launch was thus held immovable and safe from injury. In the meanwhile, Alvin had employed himself in shutting down the motor, turning off the gasoline and air tank valves and making ready to leave the launch in its usual good order.

Mike said:

"I have a brilliant suggistion to make to ye, as me uncle said when he arranged to foight six men, by taking on one each day instead of engaging them all at once. The same is that we indoolge in our noon repast on shore."

The plans of the lads when they left home was to have dinner at the hotel in Wiscasset, but they had been so delayed by their leisurely ascent of the river that the meridian was past. A supply of sandwiches, ginger ale and sarsaparilla was laid in so as to be prepared for contingencies, and it need not be said that all had keen appetites. Chester remarked that it was only a brief run to the little town ahead. Moreover, it was more convenient to eat on the launch, where they could spread the food on one of the seats or the cover of the cockpit. But every boy would rather chew a venison or bear steak, though tough as leather, in preference to a tender, juicy bit of beef, and eating in the woods is tenfold more enticing than in a house or on a boat. Besides, they had been sitting so long that the change would be a relief. Accordingly, Chester and Mike gathered up the big paper bags which held the lunch, and the bottles of soft stuff, and leaped lightly ashore.

The little party walked the short distance to the primitive blockhouse, and passing a little way beyond sat down on the pine burrs and grass and tackled the food. The clear air, the odorous breath of the forest, and the soft ripple of the stream flowing past, gave the repast a charm beyond that which the Waldorf-Astoria can impart to its guests.

"It makes me sigh," said Mike when the last morsel of food had disappeared and he drew the napkin across his lips, "to think that only a few waaks are lift to us of this bliss of life."

"Yes," replied Captain Alvin; "the days fly fast; soon I shall have to go back to school and study so hard there will be mighty little time left for play."

"The same here," added Chester in a lugubrious voice. "I don't suppose there would be half as much fun in this sport if we took it straight along."

"I'm willing to try the same for tin or twinty years; it's mesilf that doesn't belave I'd grow weary in less time than thot. Couldn't ye persuade your dad, you j'ining company wid him, Chister, to give the thing a thrial for that long?"

Alvin shook his head.

"Suppose our parents should be so foolish, do you think your father and mother would allow you to squander your time like that?"

Mike removed his cap and scratched his head.

"I'm afeard there'd be objiction from that side of the house. Ye see that twenty years from now dad, if he's alive, which God grant, will be an old man; thrue I'd be in me prime, and if he was too overbearing wid me, I could lay him over me knee and spank him, but I'd sorter hate to do that, bekase of the kindness he had shown me in days gone by. Besides," added Mike, with a big wink, "me mither would be sure to take dad's part, and I'm convinced that twenty years from now she'll be bigger and stronger than to-day. With the two united in battle array agin me, I'd hev no ch'ice but to take to the woods. Yes; we'll have to give up the idea which sthruck me so favorable at first. What do ye intind to do with the Deerfoot, Captain, when the summer is gone?"

"Draw her out on land and cover her with canvas for the winter, so as to keep her in condition for a bigger outing next year."

"That maans, I 'spose, ye'll carry her in the house and put her to bed and kiver her up the same as a sick baby?"

"Hardly that, but she will need and will receive the best of care—hark!"

The three were silent for a minute. Faintly but distinctly all caught the distant whirr from the exhaust of a speed launch. They quickly noted that the sound grew less audible—proof that the launch was speeding away from them.

At first it seemed to be in the direction of Wiscasset, but when they were barely able to hear the noise, they agreed that it was from down the river. Inasmuch as they had not met any boat on their way to this point, they were puzzled to understand how the craft could have passed them without being seen. The only explanation was that it had come nearly to the blockhouse from below, and then owing to some cause had turned about and gone back.

"That's queer," remarked Alvin, as a sudden suspicion flashed over him. He sprang to his feet and ran round the building, the others at his heels, for the same dread was with them. In a moment Alvin halted with the exclamation:

"Someone has run off with our launch!"

Such was the fact.

CHAPTER XII. In the Telegraph Office

"Maybe it slipped free and floated off," said Chester, who did not pause until he reached the water's edge.

"Mebbe she climbed out of the river and wint round t'other side of the blockhouse," suggested Mike, who regretted the next moment his ill-timed jest and joined Chester, with Alvin only a pace or two behind them.

There was a brief hope that Chester was right and that the motor boat had worked free and drifted down stream, but it was quickly evident that that was impossible. The bow line and anchor would have held if not disturbed by someone.

Then, too, what meant the muffled exhaust heard a few minutes before? It could have been caused only by the starting of the motor. Alvin, who showed quicker wit than his companions, examined the ground at the water's edge. He quickly read the solution.

"There are the footprints of several people in the soft earth. All is as plain as day."

"All what?" asked Chester.

"The manner of the Deerfoot's going."

"Give us your explanation."

"While we sat behind the blockhouse eating lunch, two or three or perhaps more persons came out of the woods and walked to this spot; they cast off the bow line, sprang aboard; one of them drew the boat out over the stern anchor and tripped it; they did not start the engine till they had drifted round the bend below; then they headed for Sheepscot Bay and are well on their way there, running at full speed as they do not need to spare the launch."

"Bedad! I b'lave ye're right," said Mike, compressing his lips. "I'm off!"

"What do you mean?" asked the astonished Captain.

"I'm going to run a race wid the same to Cape Newagen!"

"Why, you have no more chance of overtaking the boat than you have of out-swimming the Mauretania."

But Mike made no reply. Spitting on his hands and rubbing them together, he broke into a lope and quickly passed from sight in the woods.

Despite the alarming situation, Alvin and Chester looked in each other's face and laughed.

"Did you ever know of anything so crazy?" asked the Captain.

"Never; the idea of putting his short legs against a boat that can run twenty odd miles an hour and has a good start, is worthy of Mike Murphy alone."

"But we must do something," said the puzzled Alvin; "someone has stolen the launch and should be headed off."

"How shall we do it?"

"The easiest way is to cross the long bridge to Wiscasset on the other side of the river and telegraph to different points down stream."

They were about to start when Alvin said:

"I ought not to have allowed Mike to go off as he did. He is so rash and headlong that he will be sure to run into trouble. If we go to Wiscasset, we shall be separated so long that we shall lose him altogether. If I had only put the switch plug in my pocket they could not have started the motor without a lot of time and trouble!"

"Why not follow him down stream?"

"That plan was in my mind. The boat hasn't had time to go far. Suppose we try Point Quarry. That is the lowest village of Edgecomb township, where Cross River turns off and runs into the Back River, which follows the course of the Sheepscot and joins it lower down. At Point Quarry the stream is so narrow that the Deerfoot is sure to be seen."

"Provided someone happens to be looking."

"Many of these small places have telegraph lines open in the summer, but are closed in winter. A road leads from Charmount to Point Quarry, which isn't more than four or five miles away. Less than half of that distance will take us to Charmount. Come on."

The boys lost no time. Both had studied their map so closely before leaving home and on their way up the Sheepscot that they had no fear of going astray. The surrounding country is sparsely settled, with prosperous farms here and there lining the highway. The walking was good and the sky had cleared within the last few hours. The lads were athletic, and were impelled by impatience and resentment toward whoever had taken such a liberty with another's property.

Two miles took them to a point where a branch road led off at right angles in the direction of the Sheepscot and consequently to the meager settlement of Charmount, below the eddy, where a wooden bridge joins the mainland to Davis Island. They met no vehicles or footmen, though they passed a number of tidy looking houses and saw men at work in the fields. Their destination was less than a mile off and they reached it in due time. They found a young woman in charge of the telegraph instrument, who in answer to their inquiry said she could send a message to Point Quarry, where the station would be closed in a few weeks.

The youths while on the road had formulated what to say by telegraph. Since they had no acquaintance at either place, Alvin addressed his inquiry to the operator, who happened also to be a young woman. This was the message:

"Will you be good enough to tell me, if you can, whether a motor boat has passed down the river within the last few minutes?"

In a brief while, an unexpectedly favorable reply was returned. It was addressed, however, to the young woman herself, who after writing it down rose to her feet and called to Alvin.

"Here is your answer. Miss Prentiss says that it isn't her business to keep watch of boats passing up and down stream, her salary being so big that she has no time to give attention to anything except the affairs of her office."

"I suppose that is meant as sarcasm," commented Alvin.

"It does sound like it, but she adds that the fisherman, Pete Davis, came into the office directly after your message reached her, and she asked him your question. He told her that such a boat as you speak of had gone past under full speed only a few minutes before and he read the name Deerfoot on her bow."

"That's it!" exclaimed Alvin. "Did the fisherman say anything more?"

"Probably he did, but Miss Prentiss hasn't reported it. Is there anything further I can do for you?"

"Nothing—thank you."

As he spoke, he passed a half dollar tip to her, whereupon she beamingly expressed her gratitude. In truth she was so pleased that she smiled more broadly than ever into the handsome face of the youth before her. Alvin suspected she was ready for a mild flirtation, but he was in no mood for such frivolity and was about to turn away, when Chester spoke in a low voice:

"She has something more to say to you."

"Well?" he remarked inquiringly, returning the sunny gaze of the young woman.

"Do you know anyone by the name of Mike Murphy?"

Alvin laughed.

"I rather think we do; he came up on the boat with us, and is rushing down the river in the hope of overtaking it."

"Well, he stopped in here and sent a telegram about it."

"Is it possible? Let me see it."

She shook her head.

"Not without an order from court; the rules do not permit anything of that kind."

"We won't tell anybody."

"I know you won't, for you will never have anything to tell."

She turned and looked down at the last sheet of yellow paper on her file. Then she grew red in the face and shook with mirth.

"To whom did Mike send his message?"

"I wish I dare tell you; it is the funniest thing that has ever happened in the office since I have been here. You couldn't guess in ten years."

"We have hardly that much time to spend in trying, so we shall have to give it up."

"When you see your friend say to him from me that his message was forwarded just as he directed."

"Where did he tell you to deliver the reply?"

"He said nothing of that. I have a suspicion that there won't be any reply to his telegram."

Alvin was turning away again, when the miss, leaning on her desk and tapping her pretty white teeth with the end of her lead pencil smilingly asked:

"Would you really like to see Mike Murphy's telegram?"

"It would be of great help to us in our search for the stolen boat," replied Alvin, stepping closer to her.

Chester remained standing by the outer door, with hands thrust in his pockets. He read the signs aright.

"She has taken a fancy to him," he reflected, "and as there doesn't happen to be much business on hand just now is disposed to flirt a little, but Alvin isn't."

"How much will you pay for a sight of the message?"

"Anything in reason."

"And you will never, never, never tell?"

"I give you my pledge that I will not whisper it to any person."

"How about your friend back there? He has a hangdog look which I don't like."

"I'll answer for him; there are worse fellows, though not many. Chester!" commanded Alvin, turning abruptly upon him, "get out of sight and wait for me."

"Yes, sir," meekly answered the youth, turning about and passing into the open air, where he added to himself, with a broader grin than before:

"He doesn't suspect she's kidding him, but that's what she's doing."

The young Captain beamed upon the miss.

"Now I'm ready to have a look at my friend's telegram."

"You haven't said how much you will pay," she replied, with a coquettish glance at the expectant youth.

"How much do you ask?"

"Is it worth five dollars?"

"That's a pretty big price, but I'll give it."

"It isn't enough."

"Name your charge then."

"Fifty thousand dollars; I can't do it for a cent less."

Alvin read the pert miss aright. He soberly reached into his pocket and drew out his wallet.

"I haven't that much with me; will you take my promissory note?"

"Nothing but cash goes here."

"Some other day—good day."

He lifted his cap and passed out doors to join his grinning friend. The two started off at a brisk pace and had not taken a dozen steps when they ran straight into trouble.

CHAPTER XIII. A Slight Mistake

An automobile chugging along at the rate of thirty miles an hour whirled around a bend in the road from the eastward and approached the youths, who halted and looked wonderingly at it. The youthful chauffeur bent over the steering wheel, and beside him sat a bearded, grim-looking man in middle life, with a big brass badge on his breast. The two were the only occupants of the car, the broad rear seat being unoccupied.

The moment the constable, as he was, caught sight of the lads, he raised his hand to signify he had business with them. At the same time the chauffeur slowed up in front of Alvin and Chester. The officer leaped out before the car had hardly stopped and strode toward them.

"I want you!" was his crisp remark.

"What do you want of us?" asked the astonished Alvin.

"I'll blame soon show you. No shenanigan! Hand over your pistols."

"We haven't any; you are the only one hereabouts that's armed," said the Captain, observing that the man had drawn a revolver.

"In here with you! I've no time to fool!"

The lads resented his peremptory manner. Chester asked:

"Why should we get into your auto? We prefer to choose our own company; we don't like your looks."

"I know mighty well you don't, nor do I like your looks, but that makes no difference. In with you, I say, or I'll blow your heads off!"

The alarming words and action of the officer left no doubt of his earnestness. Alvin replied:

"We have a right to know why you arrest us; we have done nothing unlawful."

"I don't mind reminding you that the Rockledge post office was robbed last night. Banet Raymond the postmaster said it was done by three scoundrels—all wearing masks and dressed in yachting clothes. They came this way; where's the other fellow?"

"We had a companion with us when we came up the Sheepscot, but he's gone in search of our boat that someone stole from us a little while ago."

"You're the skeezicks I'm after; we'll soon have the third burglar."

"What do you mean to do with us?" asked Alvin. "Where is your warrant?"

"I don't need any."

Neither he nor Chester was alarmed. The arrest could have but one issue, since sooner or later their identity would be proved; but the situation was exasperating, for it promised to interfere with their capture of the stolen boat or at least cause serious delay in making the search. It was dangerous to trifle with an officer who was in no mood to accept any excuse from the couple whom he believed to be criminals. He added:

"Robbing a post office is a crime against Uncle Sam, and he's a pretty hard proposition to buck against. If you have a story to tell me, I'll give you three minutes to do it in."

The two stepped beside the auto, the glum chauffeur silently watching them.

"It's all well enough for you to be so bumptious in the performance of what you may think is your duty," said Alvin, looking into the iron countenance, "but I suppose you have made a mistake once or twice in your lifetime."

"What's that got to do with this business? Who are you?"

"My name is Alvin Landon and my friend here is Chester Haynes. Our parents each have a summer home on Southport, opposite Squirrel Island. My father made me a present of a motor boat a short time ago; we have been cruising about the bay and islands for several weeks; this morning we left home with a companion, an Irish lad named Mike Murphy; we stopped at the blockhouse up the river and went ashore to eat our lunch; while we were doing so, someone ran off with the boat; Mike has gone on a run down stream to see if he can overtake it; we walked to this place and sent a telegram to Point Quarry, inquiring about the craft and learned it had passed there a few minutes before, headed down stream. There you have our story straight and true: what have you to say about it?"

"I don't believe a word of it. Anyhow, you'll have the chance to tell it in court, where you're certain to get justice done you."

The officer handed his weapon to the chauffeur.

"Keep your eye on 'em, Tim, and at the first move, shoot!"

"Yes, sir," responded the chauffeur, showing by his looks that he would have been quite glad of an excuse for displaying his markmanship upon one or both of the prisoners.

His hands thus freed, the officer ran them deftly over the clothing of each lad from his shoulders to his knees, to assure himself they carried no weapons. The search was satisfactory.

"Throwed your guns away, I 'spose. Now for the bracelets."

He whipped out a pair of handcuffs, at sight of which Alvin recoiled with a flush of shame.

"Don't do that, please; we'll give our parole. With your pistol you are not afraid of two unarmed boys."

The appeal touched the pride of the officer, who dropped the handcuffs into the side pocket of his coat.

"Of course I'm not afeared of you, but you might try to give me the slip, if a chance should happen to come your way."

"We will not, for we have nothing to fear."

"All right. You," addressing Alvin, "will sit in front while I take your friend with me on the back seat."

Brief as was the conversation between the constable and his prisoners, it attracted the attention of several men, women and young persons, who gathered round the automobile, and catching the meaning of the incident from the remarks of those concerned, naturally indulged in remarks.

"Seems to me that this part of Maine has become a favorite tramping ground for yeggmen and post office robbers," said a man in white flannels, with a tennis racquet in one hand and two tennis balls in the other. "These gentlemen have begun young."

"Who would think it of them?" asked the sweet girl at his side.

"Can't judge a fellow by his looks."

"Which is fortunate for you, Algernon."

He lifted his hat in mock obeisance.

An older man, probably a member of the same party of players, spoke oracularly:

"You needn't say that, Gwendolen; you can judge a person by his looks. Now just to look at the face of that chap on the front seat. He is rather handsome, but it is easy to see that the stamp of crime is there, as plain as the sun at noonday. Like enough he is a tough from the Bowery of New York."

"And the one on the rear seat beside the officer isn't any better," said a middle-aged woman, peering through her eyeglasses. "Just think of two as young as they robbing a post office for a few paltry dollars, and almost beating the life out of the old postmaster! Ugh! it would serve them right if they were lynched."

Every word of this and many more were heard by Alvin and Chester during their brief debate with the officer. It "added to the gayety of nations" and caused Alvin to turn his head and say to his friend:

"Give a dog a bad name, Chester—you know the rest. We don't seem to have made a very good impression in Charmount. I never knew I looked so much like a double-dyed villain."

"I have noticed it many times and it has caused me much pain."

"It might distress me, if we both were not in the same boat."

"We have often been in the same boat, but I don't know that we ever shall be again. Ah, you have one friend in Charmount."

"Who is he?" asked Alvin, with quick interest.

"It's a she; cast your eye toward the telegraph office."

As Alvin did so, he saw the sweet-looking telegraphist in the door and watching proceedings. He could not resist the temptation to touch his fingers to his lips and waft them toward her. Nothing daunted, she replied similarly, whereat most of the spectators were shocked.

"I should hold her in tender regard," said Alvin, "if she didn't ask such a big price for a look at Mike's telegram."

"How much does she want?"

"Fifty thousand dollars."

"Why didn't you give it her?"

"I didn't happen to have the change with me; can you help me out?"

"I should like to help us both out, but the officer might object."

The chauffeur was backing and turning, and now headed the machine over the road by which he had brought his employer to this spot.

"Where to now?" asked Alvin of their gaoler.

"Augusta—as straight and fast as we can travel."

But Alvin Landon and Chester Haynes down to the present time have never seen the capital of the State of Maine.

CHAPTER XIV. A Friend in Need

The automobile with the constable and two prisoners sped down the road, aiming to stride the main highway leading northward to Augusta. It was a good run, but the machine ought to make it before night closed in, for the days were long and the course was favorable. The officer could have boarded the Gardiner at one of the stopping places and made the journey by water, but nothing was to be gained by so doing.

The chauffeur slowed down and honked as he drew near the turn in the roadway. Just then he saw another auto coming from the north and curving about to enter the road leading to Charmount. It was similar to the car in which our friends were riding and held only one passenger who sat beside the chauffeur, the rear seat being empty.

Something in the appearance of the former struck Alvin as familiar. He was middle-aged, neatly dressed, with sandy mustache and slightly stooping shoulders. He looked sharply at the youth as the machines drew nearer. A moment before they came opposite, he called out:

"Hello, Alvin! Where are you going? Gabe, what's up?"

The latter query was addressed to the constable, the two being old acquaintances. Each ordered his chauffeur to stop, and they obeyed, with the machines side by side.

It was at this juncture that Chester, who was the first to recognize the man, called to his companion:

"It's Mr. Keyes Richards from Boothbay Harbor. He used to own the Squirrel Inn, but has shifted over to Mouse Island."

"How do you, do, Mr. Richards?" saluted Alvin. "We are glad to meet you."

"But I say what are you doing in this part of the world?" continued the puzzled Richards.

"Ask him," replied Alvin, jerking his head toward the officer behind him.

"Where did you pick up your passengers, Gabe?" inquired the other of the officer, who was somewhat puzzled by the turn matters were taking.

"Do you know them?" was his question.

"Well, rather; they're particular friends of mine; they are staying for the summer on Southport. Are you kidnapping them?"

"That's what he is doing," Chester took upon himself to reply.

Alvin, feeling the humor of the scene, clasped his hands and rolled his eyes toward heaven:

"Oh save us, kind sir! Save us, for he means to eat us up, and then hang us and burn us at the stake. May I not rush to your loving arms, Mr. Richards, before it is too late?"

Richards was more mystified than ever. He didn't know what to make of it all. He kept his gaze upon his old friend the officer, and waited for him to speak. The constable's face had turned crimson, for he was beginning to suspect the truth.

"You have heard of the robbery of the post office at Rockledge, Keyes?"

"Yes; I look for news of something of the kind every few days. What has that to do with my young friends being in a position that looks as if they are your prisoners?"

"Banet Raymond tells me that that robbery was done by three men wearing yachting suits. These two are dressed that way and they admit they had another chap with them, but he's run off, so I arrested them on suspicion—what in thunder are you laughing at?"

Keyes Richards had thrown back his head and his laughter might have been heard half a mile away. As soon as he could speak, he said:

"So you took those two youngsters for burglars of the post office at Rockledge! The joke is on you, Gabe, and I'll make sure all your friends hear of it. Haw! Haw! Haw!"

The poor officer squirmed and asked sullenly:

"How should I know who they were? I never saw 'em before."

"You've had enough experience to judge a little by looks; your own small amount of sense ought to tell you better than this."

"That's what I did go by. Don't you think that they look like a couple of desperate criminals?"

And the officer turned his head, scrutinized the youth at his side and then leaned over and squinted at Alvin, as if he saw both for the first time. Chester felt sympathy for the man, and waiting for Richards to recover from his renewed outburst said:

"We must be hard looking fellows, for everyone in the crowd who saw us leave Charmount agreed that we were a couple of villains."

"And one woman thought lynching wasn't too good for us."

"Well, Gabe, do you intend to carry them to Augusta?"

"Of course not, now that you vouch for them—unless they want to go there," he added.

"Can you take us with you, Mr. Richards?"

"I am on my way to Charmount to board the boat for Boothbay. I shall be glad to have your company."

"Have we your permission, officer?" asked Alvin, looking round at their guardian, as he partly rose to his feet.

The constable was uneasy. Moving about in his seat, he asked:

"I say, young men, you haven't any hard feelings agin me?"

Keyes Richards overheard the question and his waggishness could not be repressed.

"You boys have a clear case against Gabe; you ought to have no trouble in soaking him for ten or twenty thousand dollars damages."

"Is that a fact?" asked Alvin, pausing in stepping from one car to another, as if suddenly impressed by the idea.

"Gabe owns one of the finest farms in Lincoln county; you will have no trouble at all to get it from him."

The officer would have been scared almost out of his wits had he not caught the wink of Richards and the responsive smile of Alvin. The sympathetic youth replied:

"It is all right, officer, though we should have felt different if you had put those handcuffs on us. We have had a little fun and don't mind it. Good-by."

Each boy shook hands with the grim fellow, who was vastly relieved by their good will.

"You know we have to take chances now and then, but I always try to do my duty regardless of consequences."

"You have a hard job before you, Gabe, but I hope you will win; no one deserves it more," said Richards.

And the parties separated in the best of humor.

The run to Charmount was quickly made. Nearly all who saw the departure of the officer with the prisoners witnessed their return in the company of Keyes H. Richards, who was well known to nearly everybody from Augusta to the mouth of the Kennebec. He saluted a number of persons and the chauffeur who had brought him to that point circled his machine about, and skimmed off after the fleeing constable, who must have been many miles up the road by that time.

It was some minutes before the little group could understand the turn of affairs. Alvin lifted his cap to the woman who had thought that he and his companion deserved lynching and said:

"If you feel that we should be executed we are here to receive our sentence."

She stared at the impudent youngster, sniffed and flirted away without reply. The tennis player who insisted that the looks of the lads proved their villainy did not at first quite grasp the situation. He aimlessly patted his hip with his racquet and looked and wondered. Alvin with his winsome grin addressed him:

"We are unlucky that our faces give us away, but it can't be helped. The constable became so disgusted with us that he turned his prisoners over to Mr. Richards."

"Does he know you?" asked the other unabashed.

"It looks that way, doesn't it?"

"I have no doubt he was the third burglar who stuck up the Rockledge post office. You are all tarred with the same stick. However, I'll promise to drop in on you if they send you to Atlanta to keep company with Uncle Sam's guests—for I intend to make a business trip South next month."

"Are you sure it is solely on business?" was the pointed inquiry of Chester.

"That is the present outlook, but if this post office robbing industry picks up a little more, you and I might join hands and whack up."

"Chester, we aren't making much here," said Alvin. "Suppose we pay our respects to the pert young lady who rattles the telegraph key."

They walked into the little building, while Richards stayed outside and explained that the fathers of the boys owned about half the city of New York and most of the railway lines westward to the Rocky Mountains; that they would probably buy Southport, Squirrel, Outer Heron and a number of other islands by the close of next season; that their sons were two of the finest-grained young gentlemen that had ever honored Maine with a visit; that young Landon was the owner of the prettiest motor boat ever seen in those waters, and that it was stolen exactly as they had described, and he was going to give them all the help he could in recovering it. If any one of his listeners wished to earn a handsome reward, all he had to do was to find the boat. Suffice it to say, the story of Mr. Richards made a sensation, and Alvin and Chester became objects of profounder interest than when they were prisoners charged with the crime of robbing a post office.

The young heroes never heard anything of these amazing yarns, for they had entered the telegraph office to see the bright-eyed operator who had had her fling at them. She glanced up from her table as she finished clicking off a message, and remarked:

"Out on bail I suppose; the next thing no doubt, you will skip."

"Would you blame us?" asked Alvin. "The punishment for that sort of thing is pretty severe."

"Ten or twenty years, I believe."

"Something like that, with considerable off for good behavior."

"You're not likely to get any allowance for that—there's your boat!" she exclaimed, as the hoarse whistle of a steamer sounded from the river. Alvin would have liked to make appropriate reply to this irony, but really he had no time to think one up. He and his chum hurried out, merely calling good-by to her.

CHAPTER XV. A Glimpse of Something

The steamer was a small one running between Wiscasset and Boothbay Harbor by way of the Sheepscot. She rounded gracefully to at the wharf at Charmount, making fast with the ease of long habit, and amid the trucks, laden with freight and shoved and pulled by trotting men, nearly a dozen passengers hurried aboard, among them being Mr. Richards and his young friends.

Leaving Alvin and Chester to themselves, Richards entered the pilot house where he shook hands with the captain and sat down. The visitor was welcome wherever he went, for everyone knew him as among the most trustworthy of men. During the brief halt at the landing, Richards told his story to which the captain listened attentively.

"I have noticed that boat," he remarked; "she is one of the prettiest in these parts; it was a daring piece of thievery, and is sure to get the scamps into trouble."

"I want you to keep a lookout on the way to Squirrel."

"Don't I always do that, Keyes?"

"I am not certain; but a good many folks think so, and that's as good as if you really did attend to business. Now, if the launch has kept going, of course we shall see nothing of her."

"And if she hasn't kept going and doesn't wish to be seen by us, she won't have any trouble in hiding. There are lots of places where you couldn't glimpse her with a telescope. I won't forget, and will give you what help I can."

Just then the captain signalled to the engineer, the screw of the steamer began churning and she swung out into the crystalline current. Richards kept his seat behind the captain, the two exchanging remarks now and then and both scanning the water and banks as they glided past. Several times the caller slipped out of the small pilot house, and, shading his eyes with one hand, studied the shore like an eagle watching its prey. They passed small sailboats, exchanged toots with other steamers and made their landings nearly always on time.

While Mr. Richards was scrutinizing the banks, islands and the mouths of the small bays and inlets, Alvin and Chester were similarly engaged. They seated themselves at the extreme stern under the awning where the view on the right and left was as unobstructed as it could be.

They had come to the belief that the persons who robbed the Rockledge post-office included the two whom they saw at Boothbay Harbor, and that one of the couple took part in the attack upon Alvin when making his way home some nights before.

"When you remember that they were the same number as ourselves and that they wore yachting suits, it is easy to understand how the constable made his mistake."

"Not forgetting our villainous looks," added Chester.

"I understand there have been so many post office robberies in this part of Maine that there is no doubt that a well-organized gang is at work."

"And these three belong to it."

"There are more beside them. It looks as if they have divided a certain part of the State among them, and our acquaintances have been given this section. There are several facts about this business which I don't understand."

"It's the same with me. For instance, why should those fellows steal your boat? They have one of their own."

"It may be so far off that they could reach it much sooner with the help they got from the Deerfoot."

"I don't see how that can be, for they must have come up the river in their own craft and meant to go back to it with their booty. They would be sure to leave it at the most convenient place, which would be as near if not nearer than where we went ashore at the blockhouse."

"That would seem so, but if true they must have known they would add to their danger by stealing another boat. No, Alvin, we are off in our guesses."

"Can you do any better?"

"No, but you remember when studying in our school history the capture of Major Andre, that the British sloop-of-war Vulture went up the Hudson to take him on board after his meeting with Benedict Arnold. The spy would have been saved that way, if the sloop hadn't been forced to drop down stream, so that when Andre needed it, the vessel was not there. Now suppose it was something like that with these people."

Alvin thought over this view of the situation, but shook his head.

"It doesn't strike me as likely. But what's the use of guessing? The most curious part of it all to me is that they should have come along when we were sitting behind the blockhouse and find the Deerfoot waiting for them. A few minutes earlier or later and nothing of the kind could have happened. Then, too, we hadn't a thought of halting there till Mike's curiosity caused us to go ashore. Do you know, Chester, I am more anxious about Mike than about the motor boat?"

"I don't understand why."

"We are sure to get back the launch sooner or later, but, as I said, Mike is so headlong, so fond of a shindy, as he calls it, and so eager to get another chance at the fellow who ran away from him, that he is likely to run into trouble."

"He has been doing that all his life, and yet has managed to fight his way out. I haven't any fear of his not being able to do so this time."

"It seems to me that if we don't get any trace of the Deerfoot on the way down, we may as well get off at Southport and send despatches to all the points along the river, asking that a lookout be kept for our boat, and word be sent to me as soon as anything is picked up. I am not worrying about the launch, only that those villains are robbing us of a lot of fun which we counted upon."

"We'll take the advice of Mr. Richards; he may think that Boothbay Harbor, where he lives, is the best point to send out inquiries."

Now, our young friends cannot be censured because they talked in their ordinary tones, taking no pains to keep what they said from those around them. They were equally blameless in not noticing a certain gentleman who sat two or three paces away on the bench which curved around the upper deck, apparently absorbed in reading the last copy of the Lewiston Journal. He smoked a big black cigar and seemed to be interested solely in his paper. None the less, he had taken his seat for the purpose of hearing the conversation, and he did not allow a word to elude him. He wore a gray business suit, with a white Fedora hat, a colored shirt and a modest striped necktie. The face was strong, with clean cut features, and was shaven clean of all beard. His eyes were gray and his manner alert. Most of the time he held the paper so high above his crossed legs that his face would have been invisible to the boys had they looked at him. But there were three other men, as many women, and a couple of children near that were equally interesting to Alvin and Chester, who feeling they had nothing to conceal, made no effort to conceal it.

"There would be a good hiding place for the Deerfoot," suddenly exclaimed Alvin, springing to his feet and indicating a part of Barter Island, whose northern end is just below Point Quarry, from which it is separated by Cross River. Thence it reaches southward for nearly five miles, not far from Sawyer Island and the Isle of Springs.

The point indicated by Alvin was near the southern extremity of Barter Island, and was a small inlet, inclosed by dense pines on all sides, and curving slightly to the north a little distance from the stream. The opening was broad enough to admit any of the steamers which pass up and down the river, though none of them ever turns in, since there is no cause for doing so. Had the Deerfoot chosen to make the entrance, it could have been screened from sight by the turn of the small bay, and the thickly wooded shores.

As the boat glided swiftly past the boys scrutinized every part of the inlet in their field of vision, but saw nothing to give hope that it was the hiding place of the stolen launch. It was not to be wondered at, for they had already passed a score of places that offered just as safe refuge.

Neither Alvin nor Chester noticed that the man in a gray suit turned partly round, dropped his paper on his knee, and also studied the little bay upon which their gaze was fixed. He wore no glasses, for his sharp eyes did not need artificial help. Even had his action been observed by the youths, they would have thought nothing of it, for the exclamation of Alvin caused several of the passengers to take the same survey.

The steamer had hardly passed the bit of water and the boys were still standing, when Mr. Richards came out of the pilot house and hurried to them.

"Did you see anything?" he asked.

"No; did you?" asked Alvin in turn.

"I am not certain, but the captain and I caught a glimpse of something which we thought might be the stern or bow of a motor boat like yours, though as likely as not it was nothing of the kind."

"Can you get the captain to put us ashore?" eagerly asked Alvin. "I'll pay him for his trouble."

Richards shook his head and smiled.

"He wouldn't do it for a thousand dollars; there is no place to make a landing, though he might use one of the boats to have you rowed to land. He halts only at certain fixed points."

"What is the best we can do?"

"Do you mean to find out what it is that is lying in that inlet?"

Alvin replied that such was the wish of himself and his companion.

CHAPTER XVI. On Barter Island

"All you have to do is to get off at Sawyer Island, our next landing, and walk back to this inlet."

"Can we go by land?" asked Alvin.

"No trouble. There are two or three bridges to cross and you may have a little tramping to do at the end of your journey, but it is easy."

"How far is it?"

"Something like three miles—perhaps a little more."

"That's nothing for us; we shan't mind it."

"It will carry you close to darkness, but that need make no difference. The sky has cleared somewhat, but I don't believe you will have any moonlight."

"That may be an advantage; at any rate let us hope so."

Sawyer Island, possibly a tenth as large as Barter, had been in sight for some time, and the steamer speedily drew up beside the rather rickety landing. It happened that no passengers and only a few boxes of freight were taken aboard. Only three persons left the boat—the two youths and the gentleman in a gray suit, who seemed to spend most of his time in reading the Lewiston Journal. This fact led Alvin and Chester to look at him with some interest. He carried a small handbag, and appeared to be confused after stepping ashore. He looked about for a minute or two and then addressed the agent, an elderly man with a yellow tuft of whiskers on his chin, no coat or waistcoat, a pair of trousers whose tops were tucked in his boots, and a single suspender which made the garments hang lopsided in a seemingly uncomfortable manner.

"I beg your pardon, friend, but isn't this the Isle of Springs?"

"Not much," replied the agent, with a grin that displayed two rows of big yellow teeth. "This is Sawyer Island."

"My gracious! You don't say so!" exclaimed the new arrival in no little astonishment. "How is that?"

"It's 'cause it happens to be so; can't you read?"

"What do you mean by such a question?"

"There are the words painted on the front of that shanty in big enough letters to read as fur as you can see 'em."

The man glared at them.

"Was there ever such stupidity? If I signalled the steamer do you think she would come back and take me up?"

"I rayther think not, but you might try it."

And he did try it. Snatching off his hat he swung it over his head and shouted at the top of his voice.

"Hold on there! You've left me behind! Come back!"

Several deck hands on the boat must have seen the frantic passenger, who ran to the edge of the wharf, and added his handbag to the circlings, while he kept up his shoutings. Alvin and Chester, as much amused as the agent, fancied they could see the grins on the faces of several of the men on the steamer. One of them waggishly crooked a forefinger as an invitation for him to come aboard, but none the less the boat steamed straight on to the Isle of Springs.

"You might swim, stranger," suggested the agent.

Ignoring the sarcasm, the other asked:

"Can't I hire a boat to take me across?"

"No diffikilty if you've got money."

By this time the youths felt that they had had enough of the scene, and turned to follow the road nearly to the other side of the island, where it joined the one leading to Hodgdon Island and then extended across that to the bridge connection with Barter. They had made so careful a study of the map that they had no fear of going wrong. They might not have been in such haste, had not the afternoon been drawing to a close and night certain to be near when they should reach their destination.

The day was comparatively cool, for be it remembered that while we are smothering with summer heat in States farther south, there is little of it on the coast of Maine, except occasionally during the middle of the day.

Something more than half a mile brought the youths to the first turn, when they went due north to the skeleton-like bridge which joins the two islands that have been named. They had walked so briskly that upon reaching the farther end they paused for a brief breathing spell. Naturally they looked about them—across the comparatively narrow strait to Hodgdon Island, to the right toward the mainland, and westward in the direction of the Sheepscot River. Leaning against the railing, they next gazed back over the bridge which they had just trodden. At the end was a man resting like themselves and in the same attitude.

"It's odd that he is the first person we have seen since we started," remarked Alvin. "Since we didn't meet him he must be going the same way as ourselves."

"Neither of us is doing much going just now," said Chester. "Have you thought, Alvin, that we haven't a pistol between us?"

"What of it?"

"We may need it before we are through with this business."

"I remember father telling me that when he was a young man he visited Texas and at Austin had a long talk with Ben Thomson."

"Who was Ben Thomson?" asked the wondering Chester.

"One of the greatest desperadoes that that State ever produced. He looked like a dandified young clerk or preacher, but it was said of him that in all his career he never missed the man at whom he fired. The governor found him a pleasant fellow to talk with and they became quite chummy. When asked his advice about carrying a revolver, Ben told him never to do it—at least while in Texas. 'If you do,' said Ben, 'it will be the death of you as sure as you are now alive. You can't draw half as quick as the bad men whom you are likely to run against, and the fact that you are carrying a gun will bring the other's acquittal in any court where the case may be tried. But if you are unarmed, no one will molest you, for only the meanest coward will attack an unarmed man.' Now, what I think is, that we are safer without a revolver than with one. Neither of us is an expert and we should have no show with these post office robbers if we got into a fight where guns were used."

Chester was not satisfied with this view of the situation.

"From what I have heard, such persons don't wait to find out whether another is armed before firing upon him, and in spite of what you say, I wish I had a loaded Smith and Wesson, or a Colt in my hip pocket."

"Well, you haven't nor have I. The governor has no patience with this fashion among boys of carrying deadly weapons. The temptation to use them when there is no need is too great."

Chester shook his head in dissent, and as they resumed their walk discussed the near future, for it was prudent to do so. After they had crossed the second bridge at the northern end of Hodgdon Island, he said:

"It can't be much farther to that inlet where we may or may not find the Deerfoot. It is time we made up our minds what to do. Suppose we come upon your boat with the thieves in charge, shall we tell them they have been very naughty and must go away and let us have the property without making any fuss?"

Alvin laughed.

"Maybe that's as good a plan as any. I believe I can convince them that the wisest thing for them to do is to turn the boat over to us and clear out."

"If they are desperate enough to rob post offices and steal a motor launch, they are not the ones to give it up for the asking. There!" exclaimed Chester stopping short, "we forgot something."

"What is it?"

"We meant to have telegrams sent out to different points from Boothbay Harbor, asking lots of persons to keep a lookout for the Deerfoot."

"What's the need of that when we have found her?"

"It isn't certain we have found her, but it can't be helped now."

They resumed their walk, and in due time trod the soil of Barter Island, by crossing another long wooden bridge. They had met on the way a rickety wagon, a carriage and one automobile, but no person on foot. A mile or so farther they came upon a hamlet, where it seemed prudent to ask a few questions. Night was so near that it was important that they should make no mistake in their course. They learned that from this cluster of houses a single highway led to the western coast of Barter Island. Barely a half mile beyond the terminus of this road was the inlet upon which they had centered their hopes. Mr. Richards had told them that they would have to tramp this distance, but would probably find a path which would make the task easy. Although minute knowledge was necessary to enable one to speak definitely, yet Mr. Richards reminded them that the fact of there being dwellings at varying distances all along the coast proved that there must be means of communication between them.

The boys knew they were within a half mile of the inlet when they paused more to consult than to rest. The road was lined on both sides by a vigorous growth of fir. To the rear it reached several hundred yards nearly straight, but curved sharply a little way off in front. By accident, Chester's face was turned toward the road behind them. The two had not spoken a dozen words when Chester remarked without any excitement:

"I wonder who it is that's coming this way; probably some countryman or fisherman." Alvin looked back.

"I don't see anyone."

"He dodged to one side among the trees when he saw us."

"What made him do that?"

"I wish I knew."

CHAPTER XVII. The Man in Gray

Naturally the boys were curious to know the meaning of the stranger's conduct. They could not see why anyone travelling the same way with themselves should wish to avoid observation. It would seem that he would have hurried forward for the sake of company in this lonely region. Could it be he was really trying to keep out of sight?

Chester's added explanation left no doubt on this point.

"It was accidental on my part. I happened to be looking at the very point where the road makes a turn, when I caught a glimpse of something moving on the edge of my field of vision as if coming this way. Before I could do more than see it was a person, he slipped to the side among the trees. That I think proves he does not wish to be seen by us."

"He must have known you saw him."

"No; the chances were a hundred to one against either of us noticing him, though we might have done so had he come two steps nearer. Not doubting that he was secure, he whisked out of sight for the time."

"He might have done that by leaping backward instead of sideways."

"I don't see any choice between the two methods. I am beginning to suspect that for some reason he is interested in us. How is it, Alvin, that we never had a suspicion of anything of that kind?"

"Because we had no reason for it."

"Now it would be odd if that man is the one who rested at one end of the first bridge while we were doing the same at the other."

"And has been dogging us ever since. It is easy enough to find out. Come on!"

Avoiding the manner of those who had detected anything amiss, the youths faced south once more, and, neither hastening nor retarding their pace, walked along the middle of the highway until they had passed beyond the bend which hid them from the sight of the individual whose actions were anything but reassuring.

"Now!" whispered Alvin.

As he spoke, he stepped into the wood on their right, his companion doing the same. There was no undergrowth and they threaded their way for several rods and then were unable to find a tree with a trunk large enough to hide their bodies. Doing the best they could, they fixed their gaze upon the highway, along which they expected to see the man come within the succeeding few minutes.

An impulse led Alvin to glance at his watch just at the moment he placed himself behind the trunk of a pine not more than six inches in diameter. After waiting seemingly longer than necessary, he examined his timepiece again. The minutes pass slowly to those who are in suspense, but surely the interval ought to have brought the stranger into view. But he was as yet invisible. A quarter of an hour dragged by and still nothing was to be seen of him. Alvin looked across at Chester, who was a few paces off, also partially hidden from sight of anyone passing over the highway.

"What do you make of it?" asked the puzzled Captain of the Deerfoot.

"How long have we been waiting?"

"A half hour."

"Then he isn't coming," said Chester, stepping forth and walking toward the road; "we are throwing away time and it is already growing dark."

On the edge of the highway the two halted and peered to the right and left. Not a person was in sight.

"He has turned back," said Alvin.

"Why should he do that?"

"He must have known we saw him."

"More likely he dived into the wood and made a circle so as to come back to the road between us and the inlet. He can't be far off."

"He has had plenty of time to get out of sight."

"Perhaps not."

Led by the hope, the boys hastened to the next turn, which gave them sight of a hundred yards or more before it wound out of view again.

"There he is!" whispered Alvin excitedly.

"No; it is not he."

A large boy in a straw hat, with loose flapping linen duster and bare feet was strolling toward them. He kept in the middle of the road, for the walking was as good there as on either side. With his hands in his trousers pockets and whistling softly to himself he lounged forward. He started as the lads stepped out from among the trees.

"Gosh! You give me a scare!" he exclaimed with a grin. "Who be you?"

"Friends," Alvin took it upon himself to answer. "Who are you?"

"Henry Perkins," was the prompt response from the youth, whose manner showed that he was not at ease.

"Where do you live?"

"Up the road, not fur, near this end of the bridge to Hodgdon Island."

"Where are you coming from now?"

The youth hesitated a moment and then with his unrelaxing grin answered:

"I spent the day with my cousin Burt Eggles over at Westport; he rowed me across the Sheepscot, and as I told you I'm on my way hum; if I don't arriv there purty blamed soon, the old man will give me an all-fired licking."

"Did you meet anybody on the road?"

Henry Perkins shook his head several times.

"Didn't meet nobody; there ain't many folks in this part of the kentry."

"Well," said Alvin, "you may go on home now; if your 'old man' is cross with you tell him you were stopped on the road."

"Haw! Haw! He mought ask how long I was stopped. Wal, I'm off."

He strode forward with long steps, as if anxious to get away from the couple who asked such personal questions. He had gone only a few paces when he abruptly halted, looked around at the two, who were amusedly watching him, and exclaimed:

"Gosh! I furgot something—I'm sorry," he added, using the catch phrase, which was beginning to take the place of the conventional "excuse me," or "I beg pardon."

"What is that?"

"I did meet a feller a little way down the road."

The youths were interested on the instant.

"Do you know who he was?" asked Alvin.

"Never seen him afore; didn't ask his name; don't spose he'd told me if I had; I nodded and he nodded; neither of us didn't speak; that's all."

"How was he dressed?"

"Had on a soft, light hat, gray suit and carried a handbag."

"Thank you, Henry, good night."

"I 'spose I was so rattled at fust I didn't think of him when you asked me if I'd met anybody. Wal, so 'long."

"What do you make of it now?" asked Alvin of his chum, as they resumed their walk toward the inlet.

"That's the man we saw pretending to rest at the further end of the first bridge; he's the one who sat near us on the steamer reading a newspaper, and he left the boat when we did. That swinging of his hat and yelling for the steamer to come back and pick him up was a bluff. He got off because we did and he has been following us ever since."

Neither could doubt this self-evident fact, which was enough to make them graver than usual.

The man in gray must have known from the actions of the youths that one if not both had discovered him while he was passing over the road behind them. He had, as Chester suspected, turned in among the pines and made a circuit by which he came out in advance of them. This might never have become known but for the meeting between him and Henry Perkins.

But the disturbing question remained to be answered: who was he and what did he mean by his actions?

"I believe he is one of the post office gang," said Alvin.

"So do I," assented his companion; "he knew from what we said on the boat that we are hunting the stolen launch and he means to be on the ground when we find it."

"What for?"

"Aye, there's the rub; whatever it may be it doesn't mean any good to us. We have another criminal to buck against and one that's likely to get the best of us. I wish now that I had two revolvers and you a repeating rifle."

"Wishing can do no good. We'll win if we can."

It was characteristic of these two young Americans that to neither came a thought of turning back. It was more than probable that they would run into personal peril, but none the less they cheerfully took the risk.

When they reached the end of the highway which has its beginnings on the southern point of Barter Island, it was fully dark. In the single small house that stood there a light was burning, and a form flitted between it and the curtain of the window.

"Alvin, I have just found out something," said his chum.

"What's that?"

"I was never hungrier in my life."

"The same here and have been for an hour or two."

"Let's go in and get something to eat."

No railings or fence showed in front of the little faded structure upon whose door Chester gently knocked. It was opened by an elderly woman, who was engaged in setting the table. In answer to her inquiring looks Chester said:

"Good evening! Can we buy something to eat?"

"No, sir; we don't sell food; we give it to them as needs it!"

CHAPTER XVIII. At the Inlet

It was not the thin, meek-looking woman who uttered these words of welcome. The tones were so thunderous that both the lads were startled, and they did not see the speaker, until they stepped across the threshold. He was an old man, one who must have been near eighty, who was sitting near the front window, smoking a corncob pipe. His face was weazened and wrinkled, his white hair thin and his shoulders stooping, but his little eyes twinkled kindly and he wore no glasses. He was in his shirt sleeves and his waistcoat hung loosely and unbuttoned down the front. His clean, coarse white shirt showed no necktie, but there was a pleasing neatness about his trousers and thick shoes.

Alvin and Chester removed their caps and saluted the couple. The woman had not spoken and for a long time kept silent.

"Take a cheer! Take a cheer!" added the old man, holding his pipe in one hand while he waved the other toward seats; "take a couple if you like."

The wonder about the old fellow was his voice. Never had the callers heard so deep and resounding a bass. It was literally like thunder. Each asked himself what it was a half century before.

There was no mistaking his hospitality. Probably in his loneliness he welcomed any callers, no matter who they might be. He smiled upon the youths, who noticed that there was not a tooth visible.

"Bless my heart! It does my old eyes good to look upon two such handsome chaps as you! Your faces be clean, your eyes bright, you wear purty good clothes and I don't b'lieve you use terbacker."

"No," said Alvin; "we haven't begun yet."

"My! My! You don't know what you've missed, but there's time 'nough; wait till you're as old as me afore you start. How old do you think I am?"

The pleased lads scanned the wrinkled countenance as if trying to make up their minds. It was Chester who answered for both:

"You must be past sixty-five—pretty close to seventy."

The remark was diplomatic, for both knew he was a good deal older. The man threw back his head and shook with mirth.

"Do you hear that, Peggy? They think I'm purty close to seventy! That's the best joke I've heerd since I was a boy. He! He! Why, young man," he added, abruptly checking his laughter, "I'll be eighty-three come next Christmas. I was a Christmas gift to my father and mother."

"You don't mean it!" replied Alvin, with a shake of his head.

The wife paused in crossing the floor and laughed, but without the least sound.

"I don't mean it, eh? Ask Peggy."

The youths looked inquiringly and she nodded several times in confirmation, but remained mute.

"We can't doubt her," said Chester. "You are surely a wonder, Mr.———"

"Folks don't call me mister; I'm Uncle Ben—Ben Trotwood. Who might you be?"

There was no need of evasion, and Alvin briefly told all the important facts. Having given their names, he related how their motor boat had been stolen while they were taking lunch that day in the woods near the blockhouse. It was not worthwhile to mention Mike Murphy.

"Consarn such scamps!" exclaimed Uncle Ben. "They oughter be made to smart. But when Peggy opened the door I think you said something 'bout devouring food."

"We are hungry."

"Wal," said the old man, rising briskly from his chair in answer to a nod from his wife, "supper's ready and we'll all set by. If you want to please us you won't leave a crumb on the table."

"Then we'll be sure to please you."

It was a most enjoyable meal of which our young friends partook, after Uncle Ben had said grace as was his invariable custom. The food was plain but excellently cooked and there was an abundance. The host was as spry as a man of half his years, and presided, his wife pouring out tea which never tasted better to Alvin and Chester. Each of the lads, when no one was watching him, slipped a dollar bill under his plate, where it was not likely to be seen until after they had gone.

The kindliness of the old man as well as that of the mute wife made the guests feel at home. Toward the close of the meal Chester said:

"Uncle Ben, you've got the most wonderful voice I ever heard."

Plainly the old man was pleased.

"It ain't a sarcumstance to what it was when I was younger. They asked me to sing bass in the church at Trevett, but I nearly busted proceedings. The folks said that when I let out my voice, they couldn't hear anybody else in the choir."

"It is easy to believe that."

"Then," added Uncle Ben whimsically, "they made me pay for several panes of glass that they insisted my voice had broke. I stood that, till one Sunday, a boy begun yelling that he was afeard of that big black bear in the gallery and he like to have went into fits ontil I put on the brakes. Then I quit, plumb disgusted."

"Don't you find it rather lonely here?"

"Sometimes when the children wait too long to visit us."

"How many children have you?"

"Seven boys and six girls. We lost three afore they growed up."

"You are rich indeed," said Chester admiringly.

And then the wife spoke for the first time:

"We ought to be thankful and we are!"

It came out that all the sons and daughters were well married and lived within a radius of little more than fifty miles. Each family had often urged the old couple to make their home with it, but they preferred to live by themselves. There was no danger of their suffering for anything that affection could provide.

Alvin and Chester would have been glad to stay over night, as they were urged to do, but they decided to push on and learn what they could with the least possible delay. While daylight would have been more favorable, in many respects, for their task, they feared that the thieves would make off with the Deerfoot before daylight. The intrusion of the man in gray added a zest to the search that had something to do with their haste.

Since Uncle Ben rarely went beyond sight of his humble home, he could tell them nothing of the launch. He admitted that most of the time when he sat by the front window smoking, he dozed or was fully asleep. He had seen no one pass the house during the afternoon except the boy, Henry Perkins. The man in gray might have gone by, but Uncle Ben knew nothing of it.

Promising to call if they ever came into the neighborhood again, the youths bade the old couple good night. They hurried, for the wife had begun clearing away the things from the table, and was sure to discover the tip that each had left. They chuckled because they got clear of the home without such mishap.

It will be remembered that night had descended some time before, and the clouded sky veiled the moon. The path of which Uncle Ben told them was well defined, but in the dense gloom it was hard to keep it. Alvin, taking the lead, spread out his arms and swept them in front of his face to prevent collisions with projecting limbs. Once or twice he strayed to one side, but with the help of Chester regained the trail and they pushed on in good spirits, glad that they had not far to go. The temperature was so mild that they felt no discomfort from the lack of extra clothing.

As they drew near the inlet their caution increased. Alvin in front stepped as softly as an Indian scout entering the camp of an enemy. Chester was equally careful and for some time neither spoke. With the deep gloom inclosing them on every hand, they were mutually invisible.

Suddenly Chester bumped lightly into his companion.

"What's the matter?" he asked in a whisper.

"I'm out of the path again."

"I don't see that that makes any difference; we must be close to the bay. Push on!"

They felt their way in silence for a few minutes and then stopped once more. Not the slightest sound was given out by the water that was somewhere near them. Alvin hesitated, as he was afraid of a mis-step.

At this juncture, when the two stood motionless and uncertain, nature, singularly enough, came to their relief. The laboring moon for a few seconds shone partly through the heavy clouds that were drifting before its face, and the dim illumination revealed that two paces farther would have taken them into the inlet. Scarcely was this discovery made when blank night again shut them in.

"Well, here we are," said Alvin; "and what comes next?"

After all that had been said and done, it dawned upon both at this moment that their whole venture was foolish to the last degree. Suppose they located the Deerfoot, they would be powerless to do anything more. Two unarmed youths could not retake it from the thieves, and they might grope around the place for the whole night without learning the truth. If they had been able to reach the spot before night, or, failing in that, had waited till the morrow, their eyes would have quickly told them all they wished to know.

Standing side by side nonplussed for the moment, Alvin sniffed several times.

"Do you notice it?" he asked in a guarded undertone.

"Notice what?"

"I smell a cigar; somebody is near us."

Chester tested his smelling apparatus and replied:

"You are right; the odor is in the air."

"It reminds me of the kind the governor smokes; and is therefore a mighty good one."

"It is the man in gray; he smoked nearly all the time on the boat."

CHAPTER XIX. Not Near Either Bank

Having convinced themselves that the man in gray was near at hand, the next question Alvin and Chester asked themselves was whether he knew of their proximity. It would seem not, for they had moved with the silence of shadows, and spoken in the most guarded of undertones. Moreover, it was not to be supposed that he would smoke a cigar, knowing the liability of betraying himself, just as he had done. Further, there was the danger of the glowing end catching the eye of anyone in the vicinity. The youths peered here and there in the obscurity in quest of a tiny torch, but failed to see it.

While speculating over the situation an unexpected shift took place. Chester laid his hand on the arm of his comrade and whispered:

"Look out on the water!"

A point of light glowed like a tiny star from a spot directly opposite, but quite a way from shore. It was of a neutral or yellow color, and the reflection of the rays showed a few feet from where it shone above the surface. The gleaming speck, however, was too small to tell anything more.

"I believe that's on the Deerfoot!" whispered Chester.

"It may be, but it's on the other side of the inlet; we shall not learn anything more while standing here."

A new problem was thus presented. They could stay where they were until daylight told them the truth, go back to Uncle Ben's house and sleep in a comfortable bed, or pick their way through the wood and darkness to the other side of the water. After a few minutes' consultation they decided to follow the last course.

Once nigh enough to the launch to touch it with outstretched hand they would have no trouble in identifying it, no matter how profound the gloom. While each youth saw the imprudence of the action, he was impelled by the dread that the thieves would give them the slip, and be almost beyond tracing within the following few hours. If they had run into this place for shelter, there was no guessing how long they would stay.

The task before the lads was formidable. They did not know the width of the inlet around whose head they must thread their course in order to reach the point where the Deerfoot or possibly some other motor boat was lying. The distance might be brief or prove too great to be traversed during the night. None the less they decided to try it.

The star still shone a little above the silent surface which was as smooth as a mirror. The light did not seem to be far off—a fact which led our young friends to believe they would not have to walk far to reach their destination.

The immediate cause for misgiving was the man with the cigar. The most careful snuffing failed to tell the direction from which the vapor floated, and not a breath of air stirred the stillness. Whether the youths moving eastward would be going toward or from him could not be guessed. They could only trust to providence.

"The slightest sound will give us away," said Alvin as he took the lead. "Keep so near that you can touch me with your hand; I'll feel every inch of the way."

It should not be long before they would be far enough from the man in gray to move with more freedom. The plan was to make a circuit around the head of the inlet and come back to the spot where the Deerfoot nestled under the wooded bank. How long it would require to complete this semi-circle remained to be seen.

When twenty minutes had gone by and they had progressed several rods, Alvin paused and said in his guarded undertone:

"I don't smell the cigar; do you?"

Chester called his nose into action and replied:

"I don't detect any odor."

"That means we have got away from him."

"Or that he has finished his cigar and thrown away the stump. Push on."

To avoid mishap, they kept several yards from the water. The task was so hard that it would have been impossible but for the help given by the moon. The sky had cleared considerably, so that the dim light shone at brief intervals upon the water. Another blessing was appreciated by the venturesome youths. The pine woods were free from briers and undergrowth, the ground being soft, spongy and dry under their feet, because of the cones and spines which had accumulated for many and many a year. Still again, the inlet had no tributaries—at any rate the boys did not come upon any, so they were not troubled in that respect. It was simply a cove whose sole supply of water came from the broad Sheepscot.

Such being the favoring conditions, Alvin and Chester made better progress than either expected when setting out. Now and then Alvin led the way to the water's edge in quest of the beacon which had served them so well thus far. It still gleamed with a calm, unwinking clearness like the point of an incandescent light.

A gratifying discovery came sooner than the youths expected—they were turning the head of the inlet and coming back on the other side from the shore first reached. If all went well they ought to arrive at the right spot within the next half hour. They ran against an unimportant difficulty, however. A vigorous growth of underbrush clogged their progress, but having left the mysterious stranger behind, they felt no need of further care with their footsteps.

It was yet comparatively early in the night when they completed the broad half circle and came opposite the point of their first arrival. The occasional clearing of the moon had been of much help, and they had every reason to be satisfied with their progress. But before coming to a pause, they were puzzled by a discovery for which at first they could not account.

The gleaming point that had served as a guide was nowhere near them. It seemed like an ignis fatuus that recedes as the traveller tries to approach it. So far as the lads could judge they were no closer to the light than before.

"That's the queerest thing I ever saw," said Alvin, as he and his companion stood on the edge of the wood. "I thought we should run right against the boat, and now there is no chance of doing so."

"It must have crossed to the other shore while we were passing round the head of the inlet," suggested Chester, as much perplexed as his chum.

"Then we shall have to turn back."

"And have it give us the slip again. That can't be the explanation, Alvin; we should have heard the engine in the stillness. Ah! I have it! The Deerfoot is not near either bank, but anchored in the middle of the cove or beside a small island."

This obviously was the explanation, but it did not improve the situation, so far as the searchers were concerned. With the partial illumination given now and then by the moon they could not catch the faintest outlines of the boat. It might have been a dozen miles away.

"It looks as if we were up against it," remarked Alvin, with a sigh. "We shall have to wait until daylight and may as well go back to Uncle Ben's."

Chester was silent for a minute or two. He was turning over a project in his mind.

"The boat can't be far off," he said. "What do you say to my taking off my clothing and swimming out to it?"

The proposal struck Alvin dumb at first. His friend added:

"It will be easy; it won't take me long to go there and back."

"Suppose you are seen?"

"I have no fear of that; they won't be expecting anything of the kind and I shall learn something worthwhile."

"I won't agree to it," replied Alvin decisively; "it may look simple to you, but there is more danger than you suspect. No, give it up. It is my boat and if anyone chose to risk his life to recover it he should be myself, and I'll be hanged if I'll try it."

"All right; you are the Captain and I am only second mate, but it grieves me to have you turn down my proposition. Sh! you heard that?"

From the direction of the launch came the sound of a sneeze. In the profound stillness there was no mistaking the nature of the noise.

"I wonder if our friend is catching cold," was the whimsical remark of Chester; "it sounds that way," he added as the person, whoever he was, sneezed a second, third and fourth time in quick succession and then rested.

"Suppose I call to him to be careful," suggested Chester.

"Do so if you choose, but it strikes me that we are the ones who need to be careful."

"Hello! The light is gone."

Such was the fact. Not the slightest illumination pierced the gloom that was now on every hand.

"I guess they have gone to bed," remarked Chester, "and that is what we might as well do. The weather is so mild that we can sleep on the soft carpet in the woods without risk; it's a long walk to Uncle Ben's and we want to be on hand at the first peep of day."

"I can't say that I fancy spending the night out of doors."

"It will be easy to start a fire."

"And have it seen by those on the boat."

"We can go so far back that there will be no danger of that."

"What about breakfast?"

"We can reach Uncle Ben's in time for that."

"I have been suspecting, Chester, for the last hour that we have been making fools of ourselves and now I haven't any doubt of it."

"I hadn't from the first. Hist! Do you hear that?"

CHAPTER XX. A Disappointment

Through the soft, impenetrable darkness stole the almost inaudible sound of a paddle, and strangely enough, only a single stroke was heard. The listening youths agreed that the point whence it came was to the north of the islet, and it was Chester Haynes who was keen witted enough to hit upon the explanation.

"Whoever it is he is trying not to betray himself; he is using his oar as a paddle, to avoid the sound of rowing."

"But we heard him," said Alvin.

"He made a slight slip and may do it again."

They listened intently for several minutes, but the stillness was unbroken. This continued for some time, when suddenly the sound was heard, fainter than before—so faintly indeed that had not the two been closely attentive they would not have noted it.

"Another slip," remarked Chester; "I guess he doesn't know how to handle a paddle very well. But he has got ahead, for he isn't where he was when we first heard him."

"He seems to be between us and the islet."

"He may be coming this way!"

As if in answer to the thought, the few rays of moonlight which fell upon the water at that moment revealed the dim outlines of a small boat that was heading toward the very spot where the friends were standing.

"Let's make a change of base," whispered Chester, hastily turning to the north, but halting where they could see the boat without being visible themselves.

With the weak light, they could trace it quite clearly. The craft was of the ordinary structure, so small that it would not have carried more than two or three persons, and had nothing in the nature of a sail.

A man was seated in the middle holding a single paddle which he swayed first on one side and then on the other. The observers suspected his identity before the nose of the little boat slid up the bank and it came to rest. Gently laying down the paddle, as if guarding against discovery, the man rose to his feet and stepped out. As he did so, he grasped a small handbag in one hand and moved with the alert nimbleness of a boy. He was the man in the gray suit, who seemed to have formed the habit of intruding into the plans of Alvin and Chester. They waited motionless and silent until he disappeared in the wood.

"Chester," said his friend, "I'll give you eleven cents if you will explain that."

"And I'll give you twelve if you'll clear it up for me."

"I wonder now if he isn't acting as a sentinel for the others. He knows we are somewhere in the neighborhood and has set out to keep track of us."

The theory might seem reasonable to the boys, but would not hold water, for, after all, the action of the stranger did not agree with it. They felt it idle to try to guess, and gave it up. Alvin had proposed that they should stay no longer in the wood, but return to the hospitable home of Uncle Ben. Though it would be late when they reached there, they would be welcome, but both shrank from meeting the couple after the discovery of the money they had placed under their plates.

"Hold on, Alvin," whispered the other; "let's play a trick on that fellow that keeps nosing into our business."

"How?"

"Let's use his boat to get a closer view of the Deerfoot."

It was a rash thing to do, but it appealed to the young Captain.

"All right; I'm with you. We must hurry, for he is likely to come back any moment."

Had they taken time for reflection, they probably would have given up the plan, but boys of their age and younger are not apt to "look before they leap." Without hesitation, they walked to where the frail boat lay against the bank and Alvin shoved it clear. The water seemed to be deep close to land, and the Captain took up the paddle, remarking that the craft bore some resemblance to a canoe. They half expected that the man would dash forward and call them to account, but nothing was seen or heard of him, and the gloom swallowed them from sight of any person on land.

Now that the chance was theirs to settle the question which had perplexed them so long it was important to consider each step. Alvin had had experience in managing a small boat and he handled the paddle with more skill than the former occupant, for the ripple which he caused could not have been heard a dozen feet away. As the distance from shore increased, they ceased to whisper. One knew the right thing to do as well as the other, and Chester realized that he could give no directions of value.

It seemed to Alvin that since those on the launch knew the direction taken by one of their number, they would expect him to return over the same course. Instead, therefore, of making straight for the motor boat, the Captain turned to the right, so as to approach the bow or stern. Before he caught sight of the craft, he made a complete circuit of the islet, keeping just near enough to trace its outlines and that of the launch. The former was merely a mass of sand, consisting of about an acre and without a tree or shrub upon it. It must have been nearly submerged when the tide was high.

Seated in the prow of the small boat, Chester Haynes peered with all the power of eyesight at his command into the darkness, partly lighted up now and then by the moon. This made the illumination treacherous and uncertain and caused misgivings to both. Alvin glanced up at the rolling clouds, striving to avoid betraying himself to anyone on board. The presumption was that all had gone to sleep, leaving the duty of protection to their friend, the man in gray.

A look at the masses of vapor in the sky told Alvin that the heavy obscurity would last for several minutes. He dipped the paddle deeper and stole toward the bow of the launch that was beginning to show vaguely. By and by he saw the sharp cutwater rising several feet above the water, the staff with its drooping flag, and the glass shield just aft of the motor compartment.

"Sh! Sh! Back quick!"

Chester whispered the warning, and Alvin without pausing to ask the reason swung the paddle so powerfully that the gentle forward motion was checked, and the boat moved in the other direction. Two or three strokes carried it so far that the launch and all pertaining to it were swallowed up in the gloom.

Waiting till it was safe to speak, the Captain asked:

"What did you see, Chester?"

"A man," was the reply.

"In what part of the launch?"

"He was standing in front of the cockpit, about half way between it and the flagstaff."

"Then he saw us."

"No; for he was looking toward the shore to which this boat had gone. Had he turned his head, he must have noticed us."

Alvin held the reverse motion until they felt it safe to talk without dropping into whispers.

"What harm could have come if he had seen us?" asked the Captain, "I favor going straight up to the Deerfoot, stepping aboard and ordering the thieves to turn her over to us."

"Before doing so, one thing ought to be settled."

"What is that?"

"Find out whether it is the Deerfoot."

"Of course it is; what other boat could it be? We act as if we were afraid to claim our own property."

"Your property you mean, Captain. If I may advise, it is that you make another circuit around the islet and come up to the launch from the rear. I don't think there is a second man on watch, and, if there isn't, we shall be less likely to attract the first one's notice."

"I'll do as you say, though I see no sense in it."

With the utmost care the islet was circumnavigated as before, and the stealthy approach from the rear was made. Alvin depended upon his companion to give him warning, and while he remained silent the small boat glided forward like a shadow cast by the moon.

The man who had been seen standing near the prow would have been in sight had he held his position, and since he was invisible, he must have gone away. With the acme of caution, Alvin stole along the side of the launch, keeping just far enough off to avoid grazing her, until he came once more to the bow.

This period being one of the total eclipses of the moon, he could do no more than trace the outlines of the boat, whose familiar appearance filled him with burning indignation that thieves should have dared to lay hands upon it. There was not a breath of air stirring, and Chester who still clung to his doubts, now drew his rubber safe from his pocket and scratched a match over the corrugated bottom. As the tiny flame flickered, he held it up in front of the gilt letters on the side of the prow. Each saw them plainly, long enough to note that the name painted there was not Deerfoot but Water Witch!

Alvin was astounded and disgusted beyond expression. Without a word, he turned the head of the little boat toward the shore which they had left a short time before, and did not speak until they reached land. He was impatient, because he plainly heard his companion chuckling.

"Let's give up looking for the Deerfoot," exclaimed the Captain, "and see whether we can find Mike Murphy."

"I'm with you," was the hearty response of Chester.

Indeed it is high time that we, too, started upon the same errand.

CHAPTER XXI. A Telegram

You will remember that Mike Murphy, the Irish laddie, was brimful of pluck, powerful and sturdy of build and with little in the nature of fear in his make-up. His short legs, however, were not meant for fleetness, and he never would have won fame as a sprinter. When he parted company with Alvin Landon and Chester Haynes, only one purpose controlled him—that was to regain possession of the stolen motor boat Deerfoot and incidentally to administer proper punishment to the thieves who had so boldly stolen the craft.

He loped down the road, until he was panting from the exertion, when he dropped to a rapid walk, still burning with high resolve. With no clearly defined plan in mind, he turned off at the intersection of the highways, and soon reached Charmount, one of the regular landings where the little steamers for Boothbay Harbor halted to let off and take on passengers.

"The right thing for mesilf to do is to sind a tilegram," was his conclusion. "I don't mind that I ever done anything ov the kind excipt to forward one by wireless when our steamer was in the middle of the Atlantic. Howsumiver, that was sint by other folks and I hadn't anything to do wid it excipt to listen to the crackling and spitting and sparkling of the machine and to watch for the message flying out the windy, which the same I didn't observe."

His naturally red face was redder than usual, and he breathed fast, when he stepped up to the little window.

"I have a message that I wish to go over the wires as fast as lightning," was his announcement, after raising his cap and saluting the young lady.

"That's the way all telegrams go," she replied, looking smilingly up from her chair in front of the instrument.

"Thank ye kindly."

"All you have to do is to write it out and pay the cost."

"And how much will the same be?"

"That depends on the number of words and the distance it has to be sent. Write it out."

A pile of yellow blanks lay on the inclined planed board which served as a desk, and there was a cheap pencil secured by a string, but no chair. A sender had to stand while writing his message. Mike tried to act as if he was used to such things. First he thrust the end of the pencil in his mouth to moisten the lead and began his hard task.

He was so long at it that the bright young miss looked up several times to see how he was getting on. Through the narrow window she saw him laboring harder than he had ever labored in his life. His tongue was out, his eyes rolling, his cap shoved back from his perspiring forehead and he grunted, standing first on one foot and then on the other, crossing out words, writing them over again and scratching his head in sore perplexity. She made no comment, but busied herself with other work until more than a quarter of an hour had passed.

Finally the toil was over and he shoved the little sheet of paper through the window.

"Whew! But that was a big job, as me uncle said when he tipped over the house of Pat O'Keily. You'll excuse me bad penmanship, if you plaise."

The operator took the paper from him and with wrinkled brow read the following amazing effusion:

"CHARMOUNT, MAIN, Orgust——

"General George Washington,
President of the U. S. America:

"RESPICTED SIR AND BROTHER:

"There has been the biggest outrage that has happened in a thousand years. A pirut ship come up the Sheepscot River to-day and while me and Captain Landon and Second Mate Haynes—it's mesilf that is first mate—was eating our frugle repast behind the blockhouse, the same piruts boarded our frigate the Deerfut and run off wid her. If we had seen the thaives we would have knocked their heads off. Send one of your torpeder distroyers or a battleship and go for the piruts bald-headed.

"Kind regards to the missis and hoping you are well I subscribe mesilf yours with great respict,

"Mike Murphy."

The Irish youth watched the face of the miss as she studied the message for several minutes. Mike had a fair education, and although he limped in his spelling, on the whole he did well. By and by the operator looked into his face with perplexity and asked:

"Why under the sun do you address your message to General Washington?"

"Isn't he Prisident of the United States? I remimber reading the same in me school history at home in Tipperary."

"He was the first President, but that was a long time ago and he has been dead more than a hundred years."

"Then he isn't in the City of Washington, eh?"

"No, he is in heaven, where you may be sure he has a front seat."

"You couldn't forward the same to him?" asked Mike, his eyes twinkling.

"I am afraid not; that station isn't in our line, though I hope you and I will arrive there one of these days."

She drew her pencil through the immortal name.

"You wish to have this sent to the President?"

"Av coorse; what might his name be?"

"William H. Taft."

"And his addriss is Washington?"

"That's his official address, but he stops there only now and then each year."

"Where might he be now?"

"Somewhere out West or on the Pacific coast or down at Panama—in fact, almost anywhere except at the capital of our country."

"Then can't he be raiched by telegraph?" asked Mike in dismay.

"Oh, yes; all you have to do is to address your telegram to Washington, just as you have done. They know there where to find him and your message will be forwarded."

"Very well. There is the money to pay for the same."

Mike laid a silver quarter on the stand-up desk where she could reach it. But she was busy just then counting the words by tipping them off with the point of her pencil. When through she beamed upon him and announced that the cost would be a little more than five dollars.

"Woorah! Woorah! What is it you're sayin'? All the funds I have wid me is about half what you jist named."

"You can save three-fourths of the cost by striking out the unnecessary words. Let me help you."

She obligingly edited the copy. It seemed to Mike that every word was indispensable, but she convinced him to the contrary and finally succeeded in boiling down the message so that the cost of the transmission was reduced to a dollar and a half. Although, as the lad had intimated, his funds were moderate, he paid the sum and the miss lost no time in placing the telegram on the wire.

We have no record of its fate after reaching the national capital. It may have started to find the President on his never ending travels. If so, it no doubt caused him a hearty laugh, but I am afraid he speedily forgot it and the money expended by Mike was wasted.

He thanked the miss for her aid and bade her goodday. Just then the hoarse whistle of a steamer fell upon their ears.

"Phwat's that?" asked Mike, stopping short and looking at her. She glanced through the window before replying.

"It's the Nahanada on her way to Boothbay Harbor."

"Ain't that lucky now!" he exclaimed, hurrying to the landing where he joined the half dozen passengers in boarding her.

The well-known steamer Nahanada was returning from an excursion to Wiscasset, with a large party from Boothbay Harbor. You will bear in mind that Mike Murphy's departure down the Sheepscot from Charmount preceded that of his friends by more than an hour.

Now that he had time to rest and think, he did both. Like the other two youths, he chose his seat on the upper deck at the extreme rear, where he had a good view of both shores in descending the Sheepscot. He was not in a mood for conversation, and though several were seated near him, he gave them no attention. In this respect, he had the advantage over his friends, who as you will recall not only said a good many things to each other, but were overheard, as they discovered too late, by the man dressed in gray, who mixed strangely in their affairs afterward.

It was impossible that the steamer should overtake the motor boat, provided the latter held her usual speed. Mike did not expect anything of the kind, but, like Alvin and Chester, thought the Deerfoot was likely to stop on its way and wait until darkness in which to continue its flight. The thieves would know that strenuous efforts would be made quickly to recover the launch, and would try to escape recognition by the simple method named.

This was shrewd reasoning, and was justified by what followed. A few miles below Sawyer Island, where Chester and Alvin left the steamer, projects the southern end of Westport, which intrudes like a vast wedge between the Sheepscot on the right and Montsweag Bay and Knubble Bay on the left. The island is about a dozen miles long, with a width at its broadest part of three miles or so. Around the lower end sweeps Goose Rock Passage, through which boats make their way to the Kennebec to the westward. The width of the Sheepscot at that portion is nearly two miles. Mike Murphy was on the alert and scanned the shores to the right and left as well as every craft that suggested any resemblance to the Deerfoot, but saw nothing to awaken hope until the Nahanada turned to call at Isle of Springs.

Knowing nothing of interest was there, Mike rose to his feet and scanned the opposite shore. He saw a boat disappearing in a small bay, a little to the north of Brooks Point, as the southern extremity of Westport is called. He caught only a passing glimpse when the intervening land shut it from sight, but he exclaimed:

"Begorrah! It's the Deerfut, or me name isn't Mike Murphy!"

CHAPTER XXII. Found

You will remember that Alvin Landon and Chester Haynes landed at Sawyer Island and made their way to the lower end of Barter Island, where they failed to find the stolen launch. The point which had caught the attention of Mike Murphy was several miles distant, on the other side of Sheepscot Bay and half as far from the landing at Isle of Springs.

While failure attended the efforts of the couple, it now looked as if good fortune had marked Mike Murphy for its own. He waited at Isle of Springs until the Nahanadaresumed her way to Boothbay Harbor, when he looked around for some means of getting to the point on Westport which deeply interested him.

Among the loungers he noticed an elderly man, stoop-shouldered, thin, without coat or waistcoat, a scraggly tuft of whiskers on his chin, thumbs thrust behind the lower part of his suspenders in front, and solely occupied in chewing tobacco and frequently irrigating the immediately surrounding territory.

"The top of the day to ye!" said Mike, with a military salute. "Will yer engagements allow ye to take me on a little v'yage?"

The old fellow's stare showed that he did not catch the meaning of the question.

"Are you axing me to take you out in a boat?" he queried in turn; "for if you be, I may say that that's 'bout my size. Where do you want to be tooken?"

Mike pointed across the river.

"You mean Jewett Cove, huh?" said the other.

After a little further talk, Mike found that the place named was a half mile north of his destination. He explained where he wished to be landed.

"Sartinly, of course. I kin take you thar, though it's a powerful row; thar ain't enough breeze to make a sail of any use, and I don't own a motor boat like some folks round here as is putting on airs. Yas; I'll take you thar; when do you want to start?"

"As soon as ye can git ready—but howld on! How much do ye mean to charge for a little row like that?"

"A little row!" repeated the old man scornfully. "Do you want me to bring you back?"

"Begorrah! I niver thought of that; I haven't made up me mind, and ye haven't answered my respictful question."

The other chewed vigorously, spat and finally said:

"It's worth twenty-five cents to take you 'cross and fifteen more to bring you back."

Mike was astonished. Although his funds were running low, his natural generosity would not be denied.

"I will pay ye half a dollar to row me over and if ye bring me back it will be another fifty cints—but I'm not certain as to me coming back."

The trip might prove a failure. In fact the more Mike pondered the more probable seemed such a result. At the wharf a wise precaution occurred to him.

"Being as there's no saying whin I return, it will be wise for me to take along a snack of food. So bide ye here till I procure the same."

He hurried to the nearest grocery store where he bought a couple of sandwiches and was back in a few minutes.

"I should think" grinned the boatman in an attempt to be facetious, "that the best place to carry them things is inside."

"Ye're right and ye can make up yer mind that's where they will find a lodging place by and by. I'm riddy."

The old man bent to his oars and headed across the Sheepscot, leaving the islet of Whittom on the south, and aiming for a point due west of Isle of Springs. It was, as he had declared, a long and hard row, but those muscles had been toughened by years of toil and seemed tireless. The swaying was slow but as steady as clockwork, and Mike sitting in the stern admired the rower, who paused only once and then for but a moment in which to wrench off with his yellow teeth a chew of tobacco from the plug which he carried in his pocket.

The shore in front was covered with a vigorous growth of fir, which, as is so general in Maine, found root to the very water's edge. The ground sloped upward, but the height was moderate. Mike had been half inclined to direct the boatman to row directly into the little bay. This would be the quickest way to decide whether theDeerfoot was there, but he deemed it wiser to make a stealthy approach. He wished to descend upon the thieves without any notice. Besides, if they learned his purpose, they were likely, as he well knew, to elude him, as they could readily do.

Standing on the shore, he turned to the old man:

"As I obsarved, I'm not sure whether I'll be coming this way agin. Would ye mind waiting here for three or four days till the quistion is settled?"

His face was so serious that the other thought he was in earnest. Mike hastened to explain:

"Tarry until ye obsarve a motor launch comin' out of the cove; whin ye see the same, ye may go home; all ye have to mind is to wait and obsarve for mesilf."

The boatman nodded and Mike departed. He moved along the inlet, which was a great deal broader and deeper than the one visited by Alvin and Chester later on the same day. He had to thread his way for two or three hundred yards through the woods where there was no path, before turning the bend which until then hid the boat from sight. He was still advancing, all the time in sight of the sweep of water, when he stopped with the sudden exclamation:

"Woorah, now! But doesn't that beat all creation!"

Good cause indeed had he for excitement, for he saw the stolen Deerfoot not more than fifty feet away. It was his good fortune to find it with less than a tenth of the labor and pains vainly taken by his friends.

He stood for some minutes studying the beautiful model, whose name he read in artistic letters on the bow. The picture was one to delight, and it expresses only a small part of his emotions to say that he was delighted beyond measure.

No person was to be seen on board, and he cautiously pushed on until he came to the margin of the water. The boat was moored by a line looped about the small trunk of a tree, that seemed to be leaning out from the bank as if bending its head for that purpose, and by the anchor line made fast to the bow. The craft was as motionless and silent as a tomb.

Quickly succeeding the thrill of pleasure was that of hot rage against those who had stolen the boat. He was more eager to meet them than to take possession of the property. But if on board they would be in sight, for though it was possible for two or three persons to find cramped quarters for sleep, they would not avail themselves of such unless driven by necessity.

"They have gone away fur a bit," was the conclusion of Mike, who the next minute stepped lightly aboard.

"It strikes me that this isn't the best place to linger, as Tim Hurley said whin the lion jumped out of the cage after him. It isn't mesilf that has kept an eye on Captain Alvin fur the past few days without larning how to handle a motor boat."

Whoever had withdrawn the switch plug had left it lying on the seat used by the steersman. Mike thrust it in place, and going down into the engine compartment gave a powerful swing to the heavy fly-wheel. Instantly the engine responded in the way with which he had become familiar. He seated himself, grasped the steering wheel and having pushed the control lever forward waited for the beautiful craft to shoot forward. But though the screw revolved furiously the boat did not advance a foot.

"That's mighty qu'ar," he muttered, staring about him. "What's hendering the cratur?"

Still puzzled and with some misgiving, he pulled over the reversing lever. Instantly the boat drew back, but only for a pace or two when it halted again, with the prow swinging gently to one side. Then the lever was moved forward and on the instant the craft made a dive, only to fetch up so abruptly that Mike came nigh pitching from his seat.

He rose and anxiously peered around. The explanation suddenly broke upon him.

"Arrah, I might have knowed I'd forgot something, as Dennis Tiernan remarked whin he landed in Ameriky and found he had lift his wife behind in Ireland."

Shutting off the power, Mike sprang ashore, uncoiled the rope from the trunk and tossed it aboard. He sprang after it and after taking in the anchor, set the screw revolving again.

There was no trouble now. The Deerfoot curved out into the bay, and sped forward with arrowy swiftness. Feeling himself master of the situation, Mike's heart rose with blissful anticipation.

"It's the aisiest thing in the world to run a motor boat like the Deerfut. All ye have to do is to turn on the power and kaap things right. Phwat the dickens is that?"

A stone weighing more than a pound whizzed in front of his face, missing his pug nose by a half inch, and splashed into the bay beyond. He whirled his head around to learn the meaning and instantly learned it. Two well-dressed young men were standing on the shore at the spot where the boat had been moored. One of them had hurled the missile which missed Mike so narrowly, and the other was in the act of letting fly with the other. Had not Mike ducked he would have caught it fair and square.

"Bring that boat back, you thief, and take a pounding!" shouted one as he stooped to find another stone.

"Begorrah, and that's what I'll do mighty quick!" called back Mike, shifting the wheel so that the boat began a wide sweeping curve that would speedily bring her to land again. "If ye'll wait there foive minutes ye may enj'y the most hivenly shindy of yer lives."

How he yearned to get within reach of the miscreants, who stopped their bombardment as if as eager as he for the encounter!

"Have patience, ye spalpeens, and I'll accommodate ye!" called back Mike, heading straight for the pair.

CHAPTER XXIII. Captain and Mate

Mike Murphy would have given the launch a speed of fifty miles an hour had it been in his power, so impatient was he to reach the thieves who had not only stolen the launch, but had insulted and defied him. He would not pause to secure the Deerfoot, but would leap ashore the instant he was within reach of it.

Taunting and gibing him, the miscreants waited until hardly a dozen yards separated them. Then they wheeled about and dashed into the woods as fast as they could go! Though there were two and each was older than he, they dared not meet him in fair fight!

Mike could have cried with rage and disappointment. He shouted his reproaches, hoping to anger them into coming back and standing their ground, and kept the launch going until her bow nearly touched the bank. Had there been any possibility of success, he would have made after them. But they buried themselves among the trees and he never saw them again.

During those brief moments he had so plain a sight of their faces that he would have recognized them anywhere. He was surprised to know that he had never seen either before. They were not the couple with whom he and Alvin Landon had had the encounter some nights previous and who, both believed, were the thieves of the motor boat. Not to make a mystery of a comparatively unimportant matter, I may say that facts which afterward came to light showed that these young men had nothing to do with the robbery of the post offices in southern Maine, nor, so far as known, with any other crime, excepting the theft of the Deerfoot. Even in taking that they did not intend to keep or try to sell it. They were a couple of "city chaps" who, happening upon the craft by accident, yielded to the temptation to play a practical joke upon the unknown owners. Both had some knowledge of motor boating, and knowing that instant measures would be taken to recover the property, and beginning also to feel some misgivings as to the consequences, they ran into the cove with the intention of abandoning the Deerfoot, to be found sooner or later by the right parties. They were but a short distance off when the sound of the exhaust told them that someone had come aboard and they hastened back to learn who it was. Uncertain whether Mike Murphy had any more right to it than themselves they opened a bombardment, but when he so promptly accepted their challenge, they wasted no time in effecting a change of base, which carried them far beyond harm.

Convinced that it was out of his power to bring the couple to account, Mike once more headed for the mouth of the small bay. He did not forget the boatman and swerved in to where he was patiently waiting. The youth was in high spirits over his success, barring his latest disappointment, and ran in quite close to the man.

"I won't naad ye," he called, "but ye've airned yer fee all the same."

Taking a half dollar from his pocket, Mike stood up.

"Howld yersilf riddy!" he said, motioning to toss the coin to him.

The boatman sprang to his feet and eagerly held his bony hands outspread. When the couple were nearest Mike tossed the silver piece, and he deftly caught it, though the motion of the launch came within a hair of carrying the money beyond reach.

"Thank you kindly; you're a gentleman."

"Which the same is what all me acquaintances remark whin they get a squar' look at me winsome countenance," said Mike, settling back in his seat.

Now that he was once more plowing the waters of the broad Sheepscot, he spent a minute or two debating with himself what he ought to do.

"Fortinitly I haven't any Captain or mate to consult—being that I'm both."

His first thought was to head up the river in quest of his friends, but he did not know where to look for them. They would have left Charmount long before he could reach that point, and it would have taken many hours to stop at all the intermediate landings in the effort to trace them. Moreover, a not unnatural longing came over him to make the utmost of the privilege at his command. A thrilling pride filled him when he realized that he was the sole occupant of the Deerfoot, with no one to say nay to his plans. The handsome craft was obedient to his slightest whim and he could go whither he chose. The engine was working with perfect smoothness, and though lacking full practical knowledge, he believed he could run hither and yon for several days without trouble. Furthermore, his waggish disposition manifested itself.

"I might as well give Alvin and Chester a run fur their money; they let the boat get away from them and it's mesilf that has the chance to taich them a big moral lesson; so here goes, as me second cousin said whin the bull throwed him over the fence."

Midway in the channel, Mike turned the bow of the launch southward, leaving the Isle of Springs well to the left. A little later he shot past McMahans on his right, then Dog Fish Head opposite, followed by Hendrick Light, Cedarbrush Island, Cat Ledges and finally Lower Mark.

He was now in Sheepscot Bay, fully four miles across. Although he did not know the names of the points and islands, his close study of the map had given him a general knowledge and he knew precisely where he was when he glided around Cape Newagen, which, as we remember, is the most southern reach of the big island of Southport. There his parents lived and Alvin and Chester made their summer home. Running close in shore he coasted northward and soon saw plainly the dwelling of Chester Haynes, but no person was in sight. A little farther the handsome residence of Mr. Landon—that is, when he chose to spend a few weeks there—rose to view.

Mike preferred that his father should not see him, for he feared the consequences, but it so happened that the old gentleman had come down to the shore to fish and was seated on the rocks thus engaged. The very moment in which he caught sight of the launch he recognized it and rose to his feet.

"Hello, dad!" shouted Mike, waving his hand at him.

"Are ye alone?" asked the astonished parent.

"That's what I am, as yer brother said whin he fell overboard."

"Where are the byes?"

"I left them up the river; they'll be back agin one of these days."

Inasmuch as Mike showed no purpose of stopping, the father thought it time to assert his authority.

"What do ye maan, ye spalpeen, by such outrageous thricks? Come right to land, and resave the whaling ye desarve. Do ye hear me?"

"Thank ye, dad, for yer kind permission to take a sail; it's me intintion to return be morning or mayhap before. Don't worry, and tell mither I'm all right."

"Ye'll be all right whin I lays me hands on ye!"

The parent flung down his line and ran leaping along the rocks in the effort to keep abreast of the launch. He shook his fist and shouted:

"Turn into land, confound ye! I'm aching to lay hands onto ye! Do ye haar me?"

"Ye always was a kind dad and I'll bring ye a pound of 'bacca from Boothbay or Squirrel Island. Good luck to ye!"

And with a parting wave Mike turned away his head and gave his attention to guiding the craft which by a freak of fortune had come under his sole control.

"I wonder if it will be aisy to make dad think the motion of the boat raised such a wind that it twisted his words so they didn't carry right. I doubt not that him and me will be obleeged to have a sittlement and I'll be the one to come out sicond best, as was the case wid all the folks that I had a shindy with."

No wonder the Irish lad was exhilarated. He was seated in the cockpit of the finest motor launch seen for a long time in those waters, with his hands resting upon the wheel and the boat as obedient to his lightest touch as a gentle horse to the rein of its driver. The breeze caused by its swift motion made the flags at the prow and stern flutter and whip, and now and then give out a snapping sound. The sharp bow cut the clear cold water like a knife, sending a fanlike spread of foam that widened and lost itself behind the churning screw. The wind-shield guarded his face from so much as a zephyr, and the consciousness that among all the boats big and small in sight at varying distances, there was not one that could hold its own with the Deerfoot, was enough to stir his blood and make him shout for very joy.

Mike was in a varying mood. His first impulse was to make for Boothbay Harbor, but he felt some misgiving about threading his way among the many craft that are always anchored or moored there. With the steamers coming and going, he might become confused over the signals and the right of way, with disastrous results to the launch. He had not yet learned the meaning of the toots of the whistle which Captain Alvin gave when crossing the bow of a larger boat, or when meeting it.

He was only prudent, therefore, when he turned from the larger town and sped toward Squirrel Island. He observed the Nellie G. in the act of moving aside to make room for a mail steamer that had whistled its wishes, and half a hundred men, women and children were gathered on the wharf, with nothing to do but to watch the arrival and departure of boats.

There were so many constantly going and coming at the height of the summer season that the only person, so far as Mike could see, who gave him a look was Captain Williams of the Nellie G. Mike had meant to land, but he feared he would become involved in a tangle, and sheered off. Captain Williams had backed out so far that he was brought up alongside the Deerfoot. He had done so often what he was now doing that it was instinctive on his part. He could have gone through the man[oe]uvre with his eyes shut.

"Where are Alvin and Chester?" he asked from his little pilot house as he was gliding past.

"I lift them behind. If ye maat them before I do, Captain, tell 'em I've slipped off on a little thrip to the owld counthry, but will soon return."

"I'll tell them what you told me," said Captain Williams, giving his attention to his return to the wharf.

CHAPTER XXIV. "This Is Where I Stop"

Night was closing in when Mike Murphy pointed the Deerfoot northward and circled around the end of Squirrel Island, and turning eastward glided midway between it and Ocean Point, the lower extremity of Linekin Neck. He was now headed toward the ocean, and passed above Ram Island light. That being accomplished, he caught the swell of the Atlantic, long and heaving, but not enough so to cause him the least misgiving.

He was doing a very rash thing. He ought to have gone to Southport and there awaited the return of his friends, but the reckless bent of his disposition caused him to make this excursion preparatory to returning home.

"It will be something to brag about to the byes, as dad used to say whin his friends carried him home after he'd been battered up by them that engaged in a friendly dispoot with him."

He decided to keep to the eastward until clear of the numerous islands, and then make a circuit and return to Southport.

Now the National Motor Boat law contains a number of rigid requirements, of which Mike Murphy knew nothing. Such ignorance was excusable, since he had never been on the launch at night. His lack of knowledge on these points was almost certain to bring serious trouble.

In the first place, the Deerfoot belonged to what is known as the Second Class of motor boats, which includes all that are twenty-six feet or more and less than forty feet in length. Such craft are required to display at night a bright white light as near the stem as practicable and a white light aft to show all around the horizon. With these safeguards a motor boat can be easily located, except in a fog, when the foghorn must be kept going. As Mike plunged through the gloom he never thought of the necessity of displaying lights. It would be a miracle, therefore, if he was not overtaken by disaster.

And yet it may be doubted whether such a precaution would have helped him, since he was equally ignorant of the rules of the road. If an approaching steamer or large craft sounded a single blast from its whistle, he would not have suspected that it was an order for him to go to starboard, or the right, or that two whistle blasts directed him to turn to port, or the opposite direction. Such are the rules by day. For government at night, the following doggerel is helpful:

"When both side lights you see ahead,Port your helm and show your red,Green to green, or red to red,Perfect safety, go ahead.

When upon your port is seen,A stranger's starboard light of green,There's not so much for you to do,For green to port keeps clear of you."

All this, I repeat, was unknown to Mike, who having gone half a dozen miles to sea, decided it was time to circle about and return home. He retained a fair idea of his bearings. The distant glimmer of lights to the westward indicated, as he believed, Squirrel Island. Ram

Island light was nearer, and the blinking star farthest away was the government warning on Burnt Island.

All this was true, and the youth sitting with his hands on the wheel and gliding swiftly forward saw nothing to cause alarm. This self-complacency, however, was suddenly broken by the abrupt appearance of a white light dead ahead. A second glance told him it was not far off and was rapidly bearing down upon him. He swung over the steering wheel, so as to go to the right, but the next instant he saw that the big ship was still coming toward him as if determined to run him down.

The startled Mike was so rattled for the moment, that instead of using his whistle, he sprang to his feet and shouted:

"Kaap off! Kaap off, or I'll run over ye!"

It may be doubted whether his voice carried to anyone on the schooner, for none there could know that a small boat was directly ahead. Mike heard the rush of the water against her towering bow, saw the gleam of several lights, and for a moment believed it was all over with him. There were precious few seconds at his command, but pulling himself together, he whirled the wheel around and the next minute slid along the length of the black hull, so near that he could have touched it with his outstretched hand. One of the wondering crew chanced to catch sight of the small craft as it shot by and called out:

"What boat is that?"

"The Olympic just come in from Cork!"

"You fool! Where are your lights?"

"Don't need 'em. Ye may thank yer stars that I didn't run ye down and split ye in two, but don't get too gay wid me."

It was a close call. Mike remembered now that he ought to have displayed lights, but he hesitated to leave the wheel for that purpose, and it seemed to him that nothing of the kind was likely to be repeated.

"There'll be more lights showing by and by and I can git along without 'em."

He did not dream that he was flagrantly violating the law and was liable to be punished therefore. His anxiety was now to get back to Southport without more delay.

"It isn't on account of dad," he said to himself, "for he was so mad two hours ago that he can't get any madder, but it's mesilf that's beginning to feel lonely."

He had been so much interested with every phase of his novel experience that, strange as it may seem, up to this time he had forgotten the lunch which he bought at the Isle of Springs before the boatman rowed him across to Westport. Suddenly it struck him that he was never in all his life so hungry. The sandwiches were somewhat mashed out of shape from having been carried so long in his pocket, but they could not have tasted better.

"The one sad fayture about 'em is that there isn't a dozen times as many, as Barney O'Toole remarked whin he found he had only two Corkonians to fight.

"I won't say anything about this ghost of a maal whin I arrive at home, and mither will be so touched wid pity that after reminding dad to give me a big whaling she will allow me to ate up all that happens to be in the house."

A few minutes later, Mike became aware of a wonderfully strange thing: Burnt Island light instead of winking at him from the westward had danced round to the extremity of Linekin Neck, on the north. Not to be outdone, Ram Island light had whisked far up in the same direction. Other illuminations had also taken part in the mix-up till things were topsy turvy.

You know that when a person is lost, the points of the compass seem to go astray, which peculiar fact will explain the mystification of Mike Murphy. He was sensible enough, however, to know that the confusion was with himself, and he held the boat to a true course. Not long after, he was startled by striking some obstruction, though so slight that it did not jar the craft.

"And phwat could that be?" he asked, rising with one hand on the wheel while he peered into the gloom. "It couldn't have been that ship that got swung round and got in my way, and I run her down. If it was the same, she warn't showing any lights—ah! I mind what it is. The Deerfut has run over somebody's lobster pot, which the same signifies that it's mesilf that is the biggest lobster of all fur coming thus out of me road."

It will be recalled that the night was unusually dark, relieved now and then by bits of moonlight which struggled through the clouds. At no time, however, was Mike able to see more than a few rods in any direction. As a rule, he could barely make out the flag fluttering at the bow.

Just beyond the point where he ran over the lobster pot, a rift in the clouds revealed the vague outlines of a small rowboat, and the head and shoulders of two men. If they carried a lighted lantern, it was in the bottom of their craft, and Mike saw nothing of it. They were so far to the right that there was no danger of collision, and he hailed them.

"Ship ahoy! Where bound?"

"None of yer bus'ness," was the answer. "Who are you?"

"The same to yersilf; if I had ye on boord I'd hammer some good manners into ye."

These threatening words evidently scared the couple, who, not knowing how many were on the larger boat, decided not to run any risk. Mike, despite his brief sojourn in Maine, had heard of the illegal practice of many persons on the coast who gathered lobsters of less length than the law prescribes. He could not avoid giving the men a parting shot:

"I'll mind to report that ye are the spalpeens that are scooping in short lobsters."

They made no reply, for it is not impossible that the youth spoke the truth when he made the charge.

"I'm hoping that the world will soon get tired of twisting round the wrong way, for it's hard to convince mesilf that I'm not right, which the same don't often happen wid me. As I figure out it's a straight coorse to Southport. If me dad has forgot to show a signal light at home or at Mr. Landon's, I may run down the island before I obsarves the same—phwat does that maan?"

The engine was plainly going badly, and the trouble steadily grew more marked. He had not the remotest idea of the cause.

"I wonder now if the same is growing tired; I oughter been more marciful and give the ingine a rist."

He listened closely, and a fear crept into his throat. If a breakdown should take place, he would be in bad situation, not knowing what to do and far beyond all help.

Suddenly the engine came to a dead standstill. He swung the fly-wheel around but there was no response. The Deerfoot was out of commission. He sighed:

"Here's where I stop, as Terence O'Flaherty said whin he walked aginst the side of his house."

CHAPTER XXV. Good News

You will remember that Captain Alvin Landon and Second Mate Chester Haynes were disappointed, as in the nature of things was inevitable, in their search for the stolen motor boat Deerfoot, in the cove or small inlet at the lower end of Barter Island. The only glimpse they caught of a person on the launch, which bore a marked resemblance to their own, was when they first sighted the boat launch. Nothing was seen or heard of him afterward.

With the stealthy care used in the approach, Alvin backwatered until the Water Witch had faded from view in the darkness. Then he headed toward the southern shore, landing as nearly as he could at the spot where they first entered the small boat.

It would have been an advantage had they taken an opposite course, thereby shortening the distance they would have to walk, but they wished to keep all knowledge of what they had done from the man in gray, and therefore returned the borrowed boat to its former place. They agreed that it was not best to spend the night in the woods as they had thought of doing. They might penetrate to a depth that would make it safe to kindle a fire, but they were without extra garments, and now that all necessity of staying in the neighborhood had passed, they were anxious to get away from it as soon as possible. The stolen launch must be sought for elsewhere, and they were concerned for the safety of Mike Murphy, whose impulsive aggressiveness was almost certain to lead him into trouble by this time.

Accordingly, the two once more tramped around the head of the inlet, and with better fortune than might have been expected, struck the beginning of the highway on which stood the humble home of Uncle Ben Trotwood. The hour was so late that they were sure the couple had gone to bed long before, but were pleased to catch a twinkle of light from the front window, beside which the old man was so fond of sitting.

The knock of Alvin was promptly answered by the thunderous "Come in!" and the two stepped across the threshold.

"You hardly expected us back so soon," said Alvin, after the salutation, "but it was a choice of spending the night out doors or sleeping under your roof."

Uncle Ben was seated in his rocking chair, slowly puffing his pipe. Peggy his wife had finished her sewing and was making ready to go upstairs.

"Young chaps, you're welcome. I jedge you've been disapp'inted."

"Yes," answered Alvin, who thereupon told his story.

"Our motor boat is somewhere else; I don't see how anyone can go far with it, and we're sure of getting on its track to-morrow. At any rate we sha'n't rest till we have it back."

"That little boat you've been telling me about b'longs to my son Jim. If I had thought I'd told you of it, for I can see it would have sarved you well. But it's a qu'ar story you tell me. Who is that man you speak of as was dressed in gray?"

"He's one of the post office robbers, of course," was the confident reply of Chester.

"I don't understand some of the things he's done," remarked Uncle Ben.

"It looks as if he has been keeping tabs on us."

Uncle Ben seemed to fall into a brown study or he was debating some question with himself. He was gazing at the cheap picture on the opposite wall, but saw it no more than he did the other three persons in the room. His wife knew his moods and studied the wrinkled countenance, as did Alvin and Chester. Finally she ended the stillness by sharply asking:

"Why don't you speak, Benjamin? I know what's in your mind."

He pulled himself abruptly together.

"If you know, what's the use of my telling?"

"That these young gentlemen may larn, though your thoughts ain't wuth much."

He took a whiff or two, removed the pipe and with a whimsical grin remarked:

"I was just thinking—Oh pshaw! What's the use?"

He shook his head and refused to explain further. It may seem a small matter hardly worth the telling, but it would have been well had he made his explanation. The alert brain of the octogenarian had glimpsed something of which the youths had not as yet caught the faintest glimmer.

"Do you know what I think?" he asked, bending his kindly eyes upon his callers.

"We are waiting to learn," was Alvin's quick reply.

"It's time we all went to bed; Peggy will show you your room and I'll foller as soon as I finish this and a couple of pipes more. Off with you!"

The old lady lighted the candle from another that was burning in an old-fashioned candlestick on the mantel and nodded to them to follow her. At the head of the short stairs she pushed open a door leading into a small room, furnished with a bed, a rag carpet, and everything the pink of neatness. Stepping within she set the light on the small stand, and then with an odd smile on her worn countenance said almost in a whisper:

"I found what you put under your plates, but didn't let him know about it; he would have made me give back the money to you, and I know you didn't want me to do that."

"Of course not," said Chester a little taken back, as was also his companion; "that was meant for you and we wish you to keep it."

"That's what I thought. Ben is cranky. To-morrow morning at breakfast, you must be careful he doesn't catch you when you do it again. Good night and pleasant dreams."

The boys looked in each other's faces, and laughed after closing the door.

"Uncle Ben's wife is more thrifty than he," said Alvin; "but I am glad she kept the money, for she deserves it."

"And we mustn't forget that pointed hint she let fall. But, Alvin, my supply of funds is running low. You will have to help me out if we stay here for a week."

"I have enough to see us through, but I don't believe there will be much more expense on our trip home."

A few minutes later they snuggled down in the soft bed and slept as sweetly as a couple of infants.

It need not be said that neither forgot to slip a tip under his plate at the breakfast table and made sure that Uncle Ben did not observe the act. It may have been because Peggy was expecting it that she saw it and smiled. Alvin and Chester could feel only pleasure over the little by-play, for nothing could surpass her kindness and hospitality to them.

"Wal," was the cheery remark of Uncle Ben, as he lighted his pipe the moment the morning meal was over, "I 'spose you'll be back in time for supper."

"Hardly, though we should be mighty glad to come."

"I'm sorry, but you know you're as welcome as the birds in spring."

"We know that and we cannot thank you too much. I wish you would allow us to pay you something for all you have done."

"None of that!" warned Uncle Ben, with a peremptory wave of his hand. "We don't keep a hotel, and wish more folks would come and oftener."

The lads had decided upon retracing the course of the day before. That was to walk back to Sawyer Island and there take the first steamer south, keeping the same keen lookout on the way for the Deerfoot, but making no halt unless they actually caught sight of the motor boat.

The jaunt from Barter to Sawyer Island was play for two rugged youths, accustomed to athletics and brisk exercise, and was made in a little more than an hour. The day promised to be warm and sunshiny, but would not be oppressive, and they felt no fatigue when they reached the well-known landing. Upon inquiry they were told that the Island Belle on its way to Boothbay Harbor would not arrive until nearly two hours, and for that period they must content themselves as best they could.

"Why not send a telegram to Mr. Richards?" asked Chester. "He knows what we are trying to do, and, like the good fellow he is, will help us all he can. He may have picked up something worth telling."

"Mike would say, if he were here, the suggestion is a good one, as some of his relatives remarked when they were invited to take a hand in a shindy. I'll do it."

Stepping into the little post office, which reminded them of the one at Charmount and its bright young miss, Alvin sent a brief inquiry to K. H. Richards, Boothbay Harbor:

"Please let me know whether you have learned anything of the Deerfoot. I shall be here for not quite two hours.

"ALVIN LANDON."

"More than likely Mr. Richards isn't at home; he is continually on the go and may be in Portland or Augusta," said Chester.

"I think the message will catch him; I remember the bank of which he is president holds a regular meeting of directors to-day and he rarely misses any of them."

Barely half an hour had elapsed, when the young man who was the operator called to the youths as they strolled into the room:

"Here's your answer."

Alvin took the yellow slip. Chester stood at his elbow and read the message over his shoulder.

"Your boat has been found.

"K. H. Richards."

"Gee!" exclaimed the delighted Alvin; "isn't that fine? I didn't count on such good luck as that."

"But why didn't he give some particulars? He could have sent several words more without extra cost. Not a thing about Mike. We have enough time to learn something. Try it again."

In a twinkling, a second message flashed over the wire. Mr. Richards was begged to telegraph at Alvin's expense, giving fuller information, and especially whether Mike Murphy had had anything to do with the recovery of the motor boat.

CHAPTER XXVI. Disquieting News

The reply to the telegram was delayed so long that the Island Belle was in sight when the operator handed it to the impatient Alvin.

"Mr. Richards has gone to Mouse Island. No saying when he will return.

"G. R. Westerfield."

"We shall have to wait till we get home," commented Chester, "and that won't be long."

The well-known steamer Island Belle is a good boat of moderate speed, and pursuing its winding course was moored at the wharf in Boothbay Harbor before noon. The boys had kept a sharp lookout for the stolen launch, but did not get a glimpse of it. Beyond the brief message of Mr. Richards they were wholly in the dark, and since he was absent they did not know whom to question. They could easily have hired a boat to take them to Mouse Island, less than two miles away, but the chances were that when they reached there they would learn that their friend had gone somewhere else.

While the youths stood debating on the low float, they observed the Nellie G. coming in. The genial bewhiskered Captain Williams in the pilot house recognized them and waved his hand. Then for a few minutes he was busy making fast and seeing that his passengers landed safely. Everybody knows and likes the captain, and as soon as he was at leisure the boys stepped up to him and shook hands warmly.

"I'm glad you've got your boat back," he remarked, when they had talked for a few minutes.

"We heard that it had been found," said Alvin, "but we haven't seen it since it was stolen yesterday. Have you?"

"I saw it yesterday afternoon when I was over at Squirrel Island."

"Where?" asked the astonished Alvin.

"Why, I talked with the wild Irishman who had it in charge."

"Do you mean Mike Murphy?"

"I'm not certain of his last name, but they call him Mike, and he is redheaded, with the most freckled face I ever saw."

"That's our Mike!" exclaimed the delighted Chester. "Tell us about it."

"There isn't much to tell," replied Captain Williams. "I had just backed out to make room for a steamer, when I saw the Deerfoot going by and headed north. That Irish lad was at the steering wheel and was grinning so hard that the corners of his mouth touched his ears. Not seeing either of you, I asked him where you were.

He said he had left you behind, and if I met you before he did I was to say he had slipped off on a little trip to the 'owld counthry.'"

"That identifies him as much as his looks. Did you see anything more of him?"

"I had to give attention to the Nellie, but I caught sight of him as he started round the upper end of Squirrel and turned to the eastward. That's the course he would follow," added Captain Williams, with a smile, "if he meant to take the voyage he spoke of."

For the first time since hearing the good news, each of the youths felt misgiving. While it was impossible that Mike Murphy had any intention of going far out, he did not need to proceed many miles to run into alarming danger. His knowledge of motor boats was so limited that the slightest difficulty with the engine would render him helpless. He had done an exceedingly rash thing, though in truth no more than was to be expected of him. A full night had passed since he was met by Captain Williams, who in answer to the anxious question of Alvin repeated that he had not seen or heard of the Deerfoot since late on the preceding afternoon. With his usual shrewdness, he added:

"If you want my advice it is that you hire a launch and start after that boat of yours and don't throw away any time in doing so."

"Your advice is good," said Alvin gratefully, "and shall be followed."

Bidding good day to their friend, they set out to hire a launch—an easy thing to do during the summer season at Boothbay, when boatmen reap their harvest. The boys found exactly what they wanted in the shape of a 28-foot runabout, forty horse power, four-cylinder gasoline engine, with a guaranteed speed of twenty miles an hour. It belonged to a wealthy visitor, who having been suddenly called to New York on business, gave his man permission to pick up an honest penny or two by means of the pleasure boat left behind. Although such craft are easily provided with an automobile type of canopy as a protection against the weather, there was none on the Shark. But there was a plate glass windshield forward, which shut out the flying spray when the boat was going at high speed. The seats were athwartship and would accommodate four persons at a pinch and were tastefully upholstered in leather.

The young man who had charge of the Shark was glum and reserved, but inasmuch as Alvin promptly agreed to his somewhat exorbitant terms, he was anxious to oblige. Alvin thought it best to explain the situation before they started.

"George" listened silently until the story was finished, when he nodded his head:

"I know the Deerfoot; ain't a finer craft in these waters. Wish I owned her."

"When did you see her last?"

"Yesterday afternoon."

"Where?"

"Just off Southport. The Irish bonehead was talking with his father, as I suppose it was, while going past without stopping."

This was interesting information. George was asked to go first to the shore of that island, as near as he could get to the home of Alvin and that of the caretaker, Pat Murphy, the father of Mike. The run was about five miles past Mouse, Burnt, Capitol and opposite the lower end of Squirrel Island. Just to show what the Shark could do she covered the distance in eighteen minutes.

The faint hope that the Deerfoot would be found at the small landing constructed for her did not last long, for she would have been in sight almost from the first, and nothing was to be seen of her. Pat Murphy was not visible, but a few tootings of the compressed air whistle brought him from his house, where he was eating his midday meal.

So great was his haste indeed that he left his hat behind. While he was hurrying to the rocks, his wife opened the door and stood apparently motionless to hear what passed.

"Hello, Pat!" called Alvin. "Do you know where Mike is?"

"Bedad! it's mesilf that wish I did!" called back the angry parent. "Didn't he sail by here yester afternoon, his chist sticking out and himsilf putting on airs and pretending he didn't understand what I said whin I towld him to come ashore?"

"He ought to be ashamed of himself, but you mustn't feel too bitter toward him; it was the first time he had a chance to handle our boat."

"And how the dooce did he git that same chance? What were ye thinking of, Alvin, to let such a blunderhead manage yer craft? Aye, he's a blunderhead and the son of a bigger one."

"No one will deny what ye last said," remarked the wife in the door. Even the glum George smiled at the man who did not catch the full meaning of his own words.

"Wait till the spalpeen coomes home," added Pat, with a shake of his head, "and I'll squar' things wid him."

"You have seen nothing of him to-day?"

"I haven't saan a smell—bad cess to him!"

"Well, we hope to bring him home very soon."

"It's mesilf that is hoping ye'll soon do it."

Alvin gave the word to George, who set the engine going and headed to the northeast. "I wish I could find someone who met Mike and the Deerfoot after his father and Captain Williams saw her."

"I did," calmly spoke the boatman.

"You!" exclaimed the amazed Alvin; "what do you mean?"

"I saw him just as it was growing dark."

"Where?"

"A gentleman and lady took the walk yesterday afternoon from Boothbay over the Indian Trail to Spruce Point, where I met them late in the afternoon. Then the water being very calm, I went round to Ocean Point at the end of Linekin Neck, where they went ashore for a half hour or so. I stayed in my boat waiting for them, when I happened to look south toward Ram Island, expecting the light to show pretty soon. While I was staring I caught sight of your boat, the Deerfoot, heading out to sea."

"Are you sure you weren't mistaken?" asked Chester. "Couldn't it have been some other boat that resembles her?"

"I might have thought so if I hadn't used my glasses—them that are lying on the seat alongside of you. When I took a good look through them, everything was as plain as the nose on your face."

"Did you notice the one at the wheel?"

"So plain there couldn't be any mistake about it. It was that redheaded Irish chap that you've been talking about."

"And he was alone?"

"If there was anyone with him he kept out of sight."

"Did you watch the Deerfoot after that?"

"For only a few minutes; my folks soon came back, not staying as long as they intended, but when they stepped aboard I cast one more look out to sea. It was so dark by that time that I could just see the boat fading from sight. She was still headed straight to the eastward, as if the fool really meant to try to cross the Atlantic. I should have used the glasses again, but I was too busy attending to my boat. As I circled about to start for home, Ram Island light flashed out, so you can know the day was pretty well gone."

"And you have seen nothing of the Deerfoot since?" asked Alvin, with a sinking heart.

"No; I don't believe anyone else has; and," added George, dropping his voice, "I don't believe you will ever see Mike Murphy again!"

CHAPTER XXVII. An Alarming Fact

Neither Alvin nor Chester asked their companion to explain his startling words, for there was no need to do so: only one meaning could be given them.

"How far dare you venture out with the Shark?" asked Alvin of the master of the little boat.

He shook his head.

"She isn't built for rough weather."

"I know that, but the sea is unusually calm, and there isn't the slightest danger."

"Not just now, but there's no saying when a blow may come up that will swamp me before I can run to cover."

"I have no wish to ask you to go into danger and will only request you to push out as far as you are willing."

George must have known something of the youth who had hired him, that he was the son of a very wealthy father, and willingly paid a high price for one's services. The boatman scanned the sky and different points of the compass. So far as he could judge, the weather would remain fair for hours to come. In the hope of heartening him Chester said:

"With your boat capable of making twenty miles an hour, you can turn back whenever you think best and run into one of the many harbors in half an hour."

"True enough," grinned George, "if I'm within reach of 'em. I don't mind trying it a little while longer, but not for many miles."

He slowed down, for the spray dashed over the wind-shield, and it was plain the swells were increasing, or rather the boat was plunging into a region where they were growing larger.

The chums did not say anything to him for a considerable time. He could tell them nothing more and they ought not to distract his attention. They were in a fever of dread, for never before had the outlook been so gloomy for Mike Murphy. The youths even hesitated to speak to each other, for neither could say anything of a cheering nature. Alvin picked up the binoculars and rising to his feet and steadying himself as the prow rose and dived, carefully scanned the far-reaching half circle of the Atlantic. The form of a brig dimly observable by the naked eye, as it headed toward Pemaquid Point, was brought out with a distinctness that caused an exclamation of surprise.

"What a fine instrument! It equals those our government buys from Germany for the use of the army and navy. Chester, look at that fishing boat toward Inner Heron Island."

His companion stood up, balanced himself, shaded his brow and wrinkled his forehead with the strain of the attempt.

"I see the two men as plainly as if they were no more than a hundred feet away."

He slowly swept the horizon and enjoyed the visual feast to the full. Far out to sea the smoke of a steamer trailed against the sky, the hull hidden by the convexity of the earth, and nearer in a schooner had caught enough wind to belly her sails and cause her to heel over as she sped outward. Pemaquid Point showed clearly to the northwest. The fort, more than two centuries old, is at Pemaquid Beach several miles north. Nearer rose Thrumbcap Island, south of the Thread of Life ledges, Crow Island, and large Rutherford Island, almost cut in two by Christmas Cove. To the left was Inner Heron, and on the other side of the broad mouth of the Damariscotta River, the long, narrow Linekin Neck reaching northward to East Boothbay. Scanning the sweep of water to the south and west many other islands were seen—Ram, Fisherman, the Hypocrites, White, Outer Heron, Damariscove, Pumpkin and some so small that they are not known by any name.

But nowhere on the waste of heaving water did the eager eye discern the lost Deerfoot, though boats of varying sizes and models trailed across the field of vision. Alvin joined in the scrutiny, but with no more success, and was thus engaged when he became aware of a sharp turn in the course of the Shark. Looking down at the wheelman, he saw that the boat was making a circle.

"What's the matter, George?" he asked, though he knew the meaning of the movement.

"It won't do to go any farther; I've already pushed too many miles out."

"There's nothing to be gained by taking the same route back; turn south so as to pass below Fisherman Island."

"I don't see any objection to that," muttered George, doing as requested, and holding the boat to a fairly moderate speed.

The runabout was now heading southwest, with the purpose of thus continuing for a couple of miles, when she would swing round and make for Squirrel Island and so on to Boothbay Harbor.

She was still driving in that direction, when George said to Alvin:

"You have run your motor boat often enough to understand her pretty well."

"I hope so."

"There isn't much left for him to learn," was the comment of Chester.

"Take the wheel for a bit; you know the course as well as me."

"I am glad to relieve you," said Alvin, quickly changing places with the young man.

"It isn't that, but I suspect my eyes are a little better than yours; I want to use the glass awhile."

For several minutes the silence was broken only by the splash of the water against the bow of the runabout, which plowed her way with ease and grace. Chester Haynes resumed his seat and gave his chief attention to George, who was on his feet and slowly sweeping the visible horizon. The binoculars moved deliberately to and fro, with none of the three speaking a word.

By and by the young man held the instrument pointed to the north, a little to the right of the narrow fringe of islands with the odd name of the Hypocrites. He was not studying this insignificant group, but, as has been said, was looking a little to one side, toward Inner Heron, three miles away. Pausing in the circling of the glasses, he held them immovable for two or three minutes.

"It looks as if he sees something," reflected Chester, with his eyes on the man, while Alvin simply peered ahead and held the Shark to her course. George muttered something, but Chester could not catch the words. Suddenly he lowered the binoculars and asked Alvin to change places again with him. When this was done he handed the instrument to the youth, with the direction:

"Point her that way," indicating the north, "and if you study closely you'll notice something."

Without reply, Alvin spread his feet apart to steady himself and levelled the glass at the point named. The next moment he exclaimed in great excitement:

"By gracious! I certainly believe it's the Deerfoot!"

Chester sprang up and reached for the binoculars, but his chum was not ready to hand them over.

"It looks like her, but I'm not certain. What do you say, George?"

"It's her," was the ungrammatical but emphatic response.

The news almost overcame Alvin, who, passing the glasses to Chester, dropped into his seat, that he might pull himself together.

The launch was a mile off and in so plain sight that the wonder was it had not been seen before. It was headed diagonally toward Linekin Neck and seemed to be going very slowly.

"Let me have another look," said George, who retained his place at the wheel, while at the same time manipulating the instrument.

This time he did not continue his scrutiny as long as before. While so engaged, the youths used their unassisted eyes. The Deerfoot, as she undoubtedly was, could be seen in the position named, though of course with less distinctness than through the binoculars.

"She doesn't seem to make much progress," remarked Alvin, with an inquiring look at George, who swung the wheel over so as to head toward the motor boat. He did not reply to the words of the youth, to whom he again handed the instrument. Alvin persisted:

"How do you explain it?"

"She only moves as the current carries her."

"Do you mean she is drifting?"

"That's it."

A look told Alvin the young man had spoken the truth.

"That means she has broken down," suggested Chester, uttering the thought that was in both of the minds of his companions.

"It can't mean anything else," said George, who evidently kept back some of his fancies.

"Whistle to him," suggested Alvin.

A series of tootings were sent out. They were not loud, but in the stillness must have gone beyond the Deerfoot. The three listened, but heard no response.

"I knew there wouldn't be," commented George.

"Why not?"

He shook his head, but did not speak further.

After another study of his own boat through the glass, Alvin remarked uneasily:

"I don't see anything of Mike. George, did you notice him?"

George shook his head without looking round.

"What do you think, Chester?" asked his friend.

"Probably he has been up all night and has fallen asleep," was the reply of Chester, spoken with so much confidence that for the moment it quieted the alarm of the other.

"That would be just like Mike. Something has gone wrong with the engine and he hasn't the first idea of what he should do to repair it; so when worn out, he has lain down and gone to sleep. We shall have the joke on Mike when we see him."

George's lips were compressed and he remained silent until half the intervening distance was passed; then he looked over his shoulder.

"Young men, the reason you don't see Mike is because he isn't on that boat!"

CHAPTER XXVIII. The Cry Across the Waters

The words of George struck Alvin and Chester like "the knell of doom." They looked in each other's faces, white and silent for a brief spell; then Alvin whispered:

"He must have fallen overboard."

"And he couldn't swim a stroke," added Chester, in the same husky undertone.

They said no more, but, keeping their feet, stared at the Deerfoot wallowing in the gentle sea, like a helpless wreck. A faint hope sprang up in their hearts that, after all, Mike might have been overcome by sleep and would be found curled up in the cockpit. They could not see the bottom of the compartment until quite near. Then a single searching glance told them it was empty. He might have crept under the deck forward or aft, but it was hardly possible he had done so.

George ran the Shark with skill close beside the other boat. The moment it was within reach Alvin leaped across, landing on the stern, from which he bounded down into the cockpit and peered into the obscurity in front. That too was devoid of a sign of life. He and his chum were the only ones on the motor boat.

Now that their worst fears seemed to be confirmed a strange calmness came over both. Their voices were low but even, as are those of people in the presence of death.

"What do you think stopped the boat?" asked Chester.

"It is easy to find out."

His first action answered the question. A glance into the gasoline tank showed that it was empty of all fluid. The source of power had been used up.

"There may have been other causes, but that was enough," remarked Alvin. "I'll look into things on our way back."

His first plan was to borrow enough gasoline from George to run the Deerfoot on the homeward trip, but George thought he had none to spare.

"I can tow you to town," he added.

"That will do as well."

The tow-line was passed over the bow and George made it fast to a cleat on the stern deck of the Shark. Then he resumed his moderate speed toward Boothbay Harbor. It was not a long run and Alvin spent much of the time in inspecting the mechanism of his motor boat. To repress so far as he could his profound grief, he kept up a running commentary or explanation to Chester, who really did not require it, for he knew a good deal about motor boats. But he listened as if it were all new to him, and asked questions. His purpose was the same as his friend's: they talked about everything else in the vain effort to keep their minds from the awful theme that bowed them both with a sorrow they had never known before.

"If when the ignition system is in good order, the carburettor properly adjusted and the compression cocks closed, there is a lack of power, it may be due to carbon or some foreign substance on the seats of the exhaust or inlet valves. Even so small a thing as a flake of metal or of emery left from a former grinding may lodge on the valve seat or under the valve stem and cause loss of power, or a crack in the head of the piston or cylinder or a broken or worn piston ring may give the same result."

"I have heard of those and other causes," said Chester, as the two sat side by side, "but what is the most common one?"

"The valves, when they need grinding. I have not had that trouble yet with the Deerfoot, and when I do I shall not try to do the grinding myself. The work is so delicate that it should be done only by an expert mechanic."

"What causes backfiring, through the carburettor, Alvin?"

"The ignition of the gas in the inlet pipe by a flame in the cylinder left over from a former explosion after the inlet valve opens, or by too weak a mixture, by dirt in the carburettor, a leaky inlet valve, or too small a fuel pipe. I have known an open throttle and late spark to cause backfiring. If with low speed and a little more feeding of fuel the backfiring continues, you must look for carbon deposits in the combustion chamber."

"Many persons are puzzled by explosions in the muffler. Are you?"

"I learned from my instructor that they are produced by an unignited charge entering the muffler and being fired by the hot gases from the next explosion in the cylinder. This does no harm, and if the muffler is strong is a good thing, for it blows out the smoke and dirt that have accumulated."

"The trouble with—with—him, you say, was the lack of fuel."

"Yes, but he might have had plenty of gasoline and found the engine dead on his hands. Water or dirt in the carburettor plays the mischief."

And so the questions and answers went on—so many of them that you would find their reading tedious. The pitiful part of the whole business was that, as I have said, Chester could have made clear everything asked as well as his chum and the chum knew it. It was a pathetic attempt to hold their minds from the one gruesome, oppressive truth.

But they were too manly to shirk their duty. Nothing was to be gained by turning from that which sooner or later must be faced. Two of the saddest calls upon them must be answered.

"Shall we search for the body before letting his father and mother know?" asked Chester, when they had passed McKown Point and were entering the harbor of Boothbay.

"I don't know what is best. They will soon hear of it and will be frantic until the body is found."

"It is not likely to come up and float for several days, and there's no saying where the currents will take it. A few years ago a fisherman was drowned off the eastern side of Squirrel and was found a week later several miles up the Damariscotta. Someone will come upon poor Mike sooner or later, when not looking for him."

"Our search may be a short one, for I don't think the body will drift far for some time to come. We must not stop until it is found."

"Now no one beside ourselves knows what has happened except George, who is towing us. We will get him to say nothing about it, until he has permission from us. In that way the secret will be safe for a few days."

George gave his promise, and the boys decided not to make the woeful truth known to the parents until all hope of recovering the body through their efforts was gone.

For years a huge box-like structure has floated in the harbor of Boothbay, upon which is painted in big letters the announcement that it has gasoline for sale. Towed beside this, Alvin speedily had his tank filled with the fuel. The inspection which he had made of his launch showed that nothing was the matter with it, and when put to the test the engine ran with its usual ease and smoothness. He paid George for his services, taking the occasion to remind him of his pledge to say nothing about their unfortunate friend until he received permission. Then, without going to the float or wharf, where many landings are made, Alvin whirled over the wheel, turned the boat round and headed southward toward the Atlantic Ocean.

Naturally it seemed to them that their search should begin in the neighborhood of where the drifting Deerfoot was discovered. It was strange that with vessels of all kinds passing at no great distance none of them had noticed the plight of the motor boat. Had it not been taken in tow by the runabout, it could not have remained an estray much longer.

Passing to the eastward of Squirrel Island, Alvin continued southward until he had rounded Fisherman, when he diverged so as to leave the Hypocrites on his left and the upper of the White Islands on his right. This brought him into the section where the derelict had been sighted.

"Now," said Chester, who sat directly behind his chum and close enough for both to talk freely, "if poor Mike had known how to swim there might be a faint hope that he had reached one of the small islands not far off."

"I can't understand how he could have fallen overboard; it would seem that when he found himself going, he would have grasped something. He might have seized hold of one of the propeller blades."

"To do that he would have had to keep himself afloat for a brief time, and we know he could not do that."

Alvin always carried a pair of binoculars on the boat, though they were not the equal in excellence of those belonging on the runabout. Chester made continual use of these, while the Captain depended upon his unassisted eyes to scan the waste of waters. He held the Deerfoot to a low speed, for he meant to make the search as thorough as he could.

"There's no saying how far out to sea Mike went before turning back———"

"Hark!" gasped Alvin, almost leaping from his seat.

And then through the soft still air they heard the call:

"Arrah, now, ye spalpeens! Come to me arms and obsarve me give an imitation of a gintleman starving to death!"

CHAPTER XXIX. Marooned

To say the least, Mike Murphy was much disquieted when the engine of the Deerfoot stopped dead and the boat began drifting in the darkness, no one could say whither. Not knowing the right thing to do, he seized hold of the fly-wheel, swung it back and forth and part way round, and then suddenly let go, as he had seen Alvin Landon do many times. Since there was no fuel in the tank, it need not be said that this effort was fruitless.

"Whew!" he exclaimed at last as he straightened up; "if there was somebody here to tell me the right thing to do I'd do the same mighty quick, but this part of my eddycation was niglicted, as me grandmither said when the taicher asked her if she knowed the alphabet.

"I 'spose now that there be lots of handles which if I turned 'em the right way would start this old thing, but if I swung 'em the wrong way—as I'd be sure to do—I'd bust her b'iler. So I'll not try."

He sat down in one of the chairs to think, and his musings ran riot, but the end was always the same: it was utterly beyond his power to help himself out of the dilemma.

"I'll have to drift and drift till morning comes; then if I'm not too fur out on the ocean somebody will pick me up. I'm thinking the same is a good idee to lay low, as me cousin remarked whin he was knocked down. Some boat is likely to run into me 'cause I haven't any lights burning, and as she's going by I'll grab her—whisht!

phwat's that?" he asked himself, with a new thrill of alarm.

The sound that had startled him was a distinct jar of the boat. At that moment, it was so dark he could not see beyond the flag at the bow of the launch. Nothing amiss was discerned in that direction, but a second bump caused him to glance to the left, and then he received the answer to his question.

The boat had drifted against a pile of rocks, which come down to the edge of the sea on one of the two little uninhabited masses of sand and stones, known as the White Islands. This was the northern one, opposite Fisherman Island, from which it is separated by more than a mile of the sea.

The sudden discovery rattled Mike for the moment and caused him to do a foolish thing, which he never would have done had he taken a half minute for reflection. His dread was that the boat would be battered to pieces on the rocks. With no thought of his own safety, he sprang from the cockpit, placed one foot on the gunwale and leaped as far as he could, his purpose being to push the craft clear. With all his strength—and he possessed a good deal of it—he barely succeeded. He fell on his face and knees, and had he not clutched desperately and seized a craggy point he would have slipped back into the water.

What he ought to have done, as he recalled the next instant, was to use the pole on the boat to press against the rocks and shove the launch clear. That would have been easy and effective, but it was too late now to think of it.

The reactive force of his body as he leaped drove the boat back perceptibly. Inasmuch as the current had swept it forward in the first place, the action would have been repeated but for a curious condition which quickly showed itself. Had the boat struck farther south, its return after being forced away would have occurred. Had it first drifted farther north it would have cleared the islet altogether, and continued floating toward the lower end of Southport, but it so came about that when the current regained control of the launch and shoved it westward again, it just cleared the northern end of the mass of rocks and was swallowed up in the enshrouding gloom.

Mike Murphy stumbled as near as he could to the Deerfoot and stared out in the darkness. A moment after it disappeared a partial clearing of the clouds in front of the moon brought it dimly into sight again. This lasted but a brief interval when it vanished for good.

"Good-by," called the lad. "I did the best fur ye that I knowed, and now ye must take care of yersilf, which the same has to be done by Mike Murphy."

The youth was a philosopher, and with his rugged health and naturally buoyant spirits he took the rosiest view he could of his situation. It was clear that in more than one respect he was better off on this mass of rocks and sand than in the launch—that is, during the darkness. So long as he was afloat with no lights burning, he was in great danger of being run down by some larger boat. In the event of such a calamity he was liable to be caught in a crush where his life preserver could not save him.

But no such fate could overtake the lad while on the islet. The Mauretania or Lusitania or even the Olympic could not run into that collection of rocks and sand without getting the worst of it.

Now, as has been shown, Mike was really safer where he had landed, for no harm could come to him on White Island, yet his situation was anything but pleasant. He was marooned and could not leave his ocean prison without help. There was little hope of anything of the kind so long as night remained with him, but the morrow ought to bring rescue. Until then he must content himself as best he could.

But he was not the one to sit down with folded hands. Nature had gifted him with a powerful voice and he fancied he might turn it to use. A twinkling light gliding or bobbing over the water here and there showed that not all the world was asleep. His own experience told him he had neighbors. Accordingly he lifted up his voice and shouted with might and main:

"Hilp! Hilp! Somebody come to me hilp!"

He directed the tones toward different points of the compass, but a half hour passed, during which perforce he often rested, without any sign of success. And then he was thrilled by what resembled a lantern, twinkling from the direction of the Hypocrites to the westward. He renewed his call, and to add force to it, waved his arms and danced up and down on the rock to whose top he had climbed, though of course such antics were of no help.

Fifteen minutes removed all doubt. The light, sinking and falling with the moderate waves, was drawing nearer. Although his voice had grown husky, he spared it not.

"Right this way! Don't be afeard! I won't hurt ye! Hurry up, ye spalpeens!"

A hundred yards or so off—too far for him to see the boat or its occupants—the rowers paused. From out the gloom came the call:

"Hello there! What's the matter?"

"I'm shipwrecked! Come and take me off!"

The words must have sounded suspicious to those for whom they were intended.

"How came you to be cast away?"

"I landed here awhile ago and when I warn't looking me owld boat slipped from me, bad cess to her!"

This was less satisfactory to the two men, who were probably robbing lobster pots. They talked together for a few minutes, though the anxious listener could not hear what they said.

"What boat was it?" asked the one who acted as spokesman.

"The Deerfut—a motor boat that b'longs to me friend Alvin Landon, whose dad owns half the city of New York. He'll give ye a million dollars fur taking care of Mike Murphy, which is mesilf."

This announcement had an altogether different effect from what the youth expected.

"If you're worth that much we'll let someone else earn the money. Good night!"

It was an act of wanton cruelty, but it is a fact none the less that the couple closed their ears to the appeal and rowed away in the darkness. When certain that they were deserting him Mike changed the tenor of his prayer and urged them to come back long enough to receive the chastisement he was aching to give them.

It was a bitter disappointment, but the lad felt he had more cause to be grateful to heaven that he had to repine.

"I may as well make up me mind to stay here a bit, as Jim O'Toole said whin he begun his ten years sintence in jail. The weather is mild, and though it looks like rain I don't think it will come yet awhile. I'll saak me couch and go to sleep."

The danger of bruises from a fall prevented his groping long for shelter. Exposed to the open sea the islet was swept by a gentle breeze which brought the ocean's coolness with it. After much care and patience, he found a place where he was quite well screened. Passing his hands over the rough surface, he said with a touch of his waggishness which seemed never to leave him:

"This is softer than anywhere ilse, as me mother said whin she took her hands out of the dough and laid 'em on me head."

Mike never forgot his prayers, and when he lay down he was in a thankful frame of mind despite the trying experiences through which he had passed. Quite soon he was sleeping as profoundly as if in his bed at home. Such is the reward of good habits and right living.

The night must have been well along when he sank into unconsciousness. That his tired body needed the rest was proved by the fact that he did not open his eyes until half the next day was past. He felt stiff and cramped from lying so long on his hard couch, and it was several minutes before he recalled all the events of the preceding day and night.

Climbing to the top of the highest rock he gazed out over the waters. He felt no concern for the Deerfoot, which had played him the shabby trick, for if he saw it he could expect nothing from it. His most poignant consciousness was that he never was so hungry in his life. He could not recall that he had ever gone without food so long, and his craving gave him more anxiety than did the future.

In whichever direction he turned his gaze he saw small boats, schooners, brigs, steamers and various kinds of vessels, most of them too far off for him to hope to attract their attention. The nearest was a schooner, more than a mile away and gliding northward. It so happened that much the larger number of craft were heading outward. Mike shrewdly reflected:

"If they pick me up they'll niver turn round to take me home, but will speed away to the ither side of the world. I must catch one of 'em that's coming in, so he won't lose time in giving me a lift."

He picked his way to the southern end of the islet, where a broad sweep of water separated him from the other bit of land, and gazed out over the vast Atlantic which swept from horizon to horizon.

"I would display a flag of distriss on the top of a pole, if it warn't fur two raisons. The first is I haven't any pole to erict on these rocks, and the ither is that I'd have to use me own clothes for the flag, which the same would be apt to drive away all hilp."

Mike Murphy cut a strange figure, dancing, shouting, swinging his arms and waving his cap, but sad to say not a solitary person seemed to see him, or else he not did think it worthwhile to give further attention to the marooned youth.

"It looks loike it will be a failure, as Tim Ryan said whin he tried to throw the prize bull over a stone wall."

Accordingly, Mike returned to the upper end of the islet to learn whether any hope lay in that direction. His growing fear was that he was in danger of starving to death.

"Anither night will doot," he said, despairing for the moment—"PHWAT!"

The first look northward showed him the Deerfoot, speeding past barely a fourth of a mile distant. Had he not spent so much time at the other end of his refuge he would have observed her long before.

He stood for a spell unable to believe the evidence of his senses. Then, when the glorious truth burst upon him, he uttered the words that have already been recorded.

CHAPTER XXX. A New England Home Coming

The amazement of Alvin Landon and Chester Haynes was as overwhelming as that of Mike Murphy. For a brief while they stared across the water, without the Captain shifting the wheel. It is said that a person's voice is the surest means of disclosing his identity, but Mike's tones did not sound natural because of their hoarseness. There was no mistaking that sturdy figure, however, that stood on the top of one of the rocks, acting like a lunatic, as indeed he was for the moment.

The boat was brought as close to shore as was safe, where Mike stood waiting. Letting go of the wheel, Alvin stepped forward and reached out his hand, which was grasped by the lad, who leaped aboard. The scene that followed would have brought moisture to the eyes of the most indifferent spectator. Alvin flung his arms about the neck of Mike, with a fervent "Thank God!" and Mike responded in kind. Then Chester did the same, and for a moment none spoke because he could not.

"Arrah, now! Don't be childers! Brace up the same as mesilf and be a mon! Did ye iver see me betray sich foolish waakness? It's mesilf that's ashamed——"

Mike's voice suddenly broke, and dropping onto the nearest seat, he impulsively covered his face with his hands and with heaving shoulders sobbed as if the fountains of his grief were broken up. His friends smiled, but it was through their tears. The boat drifted from the rocks, and for some length of time the propeller was motionless.

Mike was the first to recover his self-control. He was laughing as with his handkerchief he wiped his eyes.

"Begorra! It's a fool that I am, as Jerry Connolly remarked whin he mistook a billiard ball for a pratie. I say, byes, will ye do me a favor?"

"There isn't anything we wouldn't gladly do for you," replied Alvin, taking his place at the wheel and moving the lever which set the screw revolving.

"Both of ye sarch yer clothes and saa whither ye haven't a few loaves of bread, some biled praties and a pound or two of maat hidden in the same."

"I'm sorry to say, Mike," replied Chester, "that we haven't a mouthful of food here on board. We have already had our dinner."

"And the only maal I've got is the one I've got to git."

"We'll make all haste to Boothbay where you shall have the biggest feast of your life," said Alvin, giving the craft full speed with her nose pointed to the northwest.

"And whin I'm through there'll be a famine started in the town, as was always the case whin dad took his dinner in any of the near-by places at home."

As the Deerfoot cut her way through the water with a speed that sent the spray flying over the wind-shield, Mike told his story, which you may be sure was listened to with rapt interest by his friends. They in turn gave him all the facts that were new to him, and each fervently thanked God for His great mercy.

The afternoon was nearly gone when the Deerfoot settled to rest beside the floating wharf, and was made fast and left in charge of the same man who had done similar duty before. Then the three walked briskly up the steps and street to the hotel.

"The bist plan will be to order dinner for the thraa of us," whispered Mike; "that will be classy."

"We have had our midday meal," said Alvin, "and the regular dinner time is an hour or more away."

"Whist now, I'll see that none of the stuff is wasted."

Suffice it to say that great as was the strain upon the resources of the hotel, it proved equal to the call, and Mike ate the biggest meal of his life. Alvin and Chester sat at the table with him, each drinking a cup of tea, but preferring no food until the usual time. You may be sure the hour was a merry one, and the guest did not stop feasting until the limit of his capacity was reached.

When they passed down the main street and turned off to the landing, it had become fully dark and lights were showing in the stores and houses. Both Alvin and Chester noted a peculiar fact: most of those whom they met stared curiously at Mike Murphy. The chums observed the same thing on their way up the street, but it was more marked on their return.

"I'm not to blame if I'm so much purtier than aither of ye, that I compil the admiration of others. It has been the same wheriver I strayed."

This was the explanation given by the subject of the scrutiny. The youths were too modest to differ with their genial companion, but the man left in charge of the boat glanced sharply at the Irish lad, and said to Alvin:

"I'm mighty glad."

"Mighty glad of what?" asked the surprised Captain.

"That that chap wasn't drowned."

"Why should he be drowned more than we or you?"

"I can't say that he should," replied the other, adding naught in the way of enlightenment. Alvin was annoyed, but said nothing further, and soon the Deerfoot, with lights burning, was gliding at moderate speed down the bay and along the eastern coast of Southport Island. There, as you will recall, were the homes of Alvin Landon and Chester Haynes, near the shore and almost opposite Squirrel Island. Chester had accepted his friend's invitation to spend the night with him. This made it unnecessary to run the Deerfoot to the shelter provided for her near the dwelling of Chester. The promise of fair weather was so marked that there was no hesitation in mooring the launch in the open without the canvas which would have been stretched over the exposed parts to protect them from possible rain.

The night was clear, with the stars shining. Later the moon would appear, but our friends were so familiar with the way that they would not have hesitated had the gloom been much deeper. They were within a mile of Alvin's home when they caught sight of the lights and outlines of a small boat on the opposite course. It was farther out than they, and they could not see distinctly until they came opposite, with barely a hundred feet between them. It was going very much faster than they themselves.

"Alvin," said Chester in some excitement, "I believe that is the Shark."

"It looks like her. What can she have been doing down here?"

Chester shouted:

"Hello, George!"

There was no reply, though the man aboard could not have failed to hear them.

"You must have been mistaken," said Alvin.

"I'm sure I was not, though I can't imagine why he didn't answer. Well, it's a small matter anyway."

Mike who had been silent for some time now spoke:

"Byes, I'm a wee bit unaisy, as Jim Concannon said whin he found his trousers was on fire at the top and bottom."

"What about?" asked Chester.

"I'm fearing that the account which dad has piled up agin me is so big that he will lack the strength to square it."

"He will be so glad to see you back that I'm sure he will think of naught else," assured Alvin.

"Whin I say to him that I didn't understand his words at the time I was sailing by yisterday and he ordered me to come ashore, he won't cridit the same. Ye see he doesn't—ah! I have it fixed!" exclaimed Mike, delighted with the idea that had flashed into his brain.

"Let's hear it."

"I'll linger behind while ye two go forrid and say to dad and mither that poor Mike has been drowned."

"Why in the name of common sense should we say that?" asked the astonished Chester.

"I want ye to break the news of me coming gintly; after they have digisted the story of me drowning, ye can say yer tongue slipped and ye meant to say I come near drowning but didn't quite make it."

"That's the most original way of telling news," said Alvin, with a laugh. "I can't see how it will be of much help, but I'll do what I can. What have you to suggest, Chester?"

"It's clear that unless we pave the way for Mike he is in for a big trouncing. I advise that he stay on the boat while we go forward and call upon his folks. We can prove to them that he has been in great danger and soften the heart, I hope, of his father."

"And thin whin the right moment comes I'll appear to 'em," said Mike, who was pleased with the scheme. "But how will I know whin that right moment arrives?" he asked.

"One of us will open the front door and whistle."

"Don't whistle too soon or wait too long, as Jack Mulrooney did whin he ate a green persimmon before whistlin' fur his dog."

Fearing that the noise of the launch might attract the attention of the father of Mike, and bring him out doors, the son curled down in the cockpit, where he could not be seen by anyone on shore. Chester sprang out and made the launch fast and Alvin followed him. Before they left, Mike raised his head.

"Are you sure the Deerfut won't play me the same trick it did last night and run away wid me?" he asked.

"No fear of that; if it does, you know how to run it?"

"Have ye 'nough gas in the b'iler?"

"Oh, keep still and don't show yourself, or I shall tell your father you are here and waiting for the licking he is saving for you."

Mike dropped down out of sight, and though he immediately thought of several important questions to ask, did not do so. He must now wait with all the patience he could summon for the signal that it was prudent for him to show himself.

It was only a brief walk to the care-taker's house, and the light shining through the window and the sound of voices told that the couple were at home. But in the very act of opening the door, the boys paused.

"What does that mean?" asked Alvin of his companion.

"I don't understand it," was the reply.

Mrs. Murphy was sobbing and lamenting like a woman distracted. Her husband seemed to be silent, as if holding himself in better control. Finally they caught some of her wailing exclamations:

"Poor Micky! The darlint is drowned and it's me heart that is broke! Wurrah! Wurrah! Woe is me!"

CHAPTER XXXI. The Man in Gray

You know there are some people who can never keep a secret. We have all met them, much to our disgust. George, the "chauffeur" of the little runabout launch Shark, was such a person. Possibly when he gave his promise to Alvin Landon and Chester Haynes not to reveal what then seemed the fate of Mike Murphy, he meant to do as he said, but somehow or other he was not equal to the task.

He kept mum on the dreadful subject until he had secured his boat and walked up the street past Hodgdon's well-known store, when he met an acquaintance with whom he briefly chatted. By the time they had finished, he had told him, under a solemn pledge to mention it to no one, all about the sad death of the Irish lad from drowning. Within the following hour this friend told the story to three others, all of whom agreed upon their sacred honor to say nothing about it to anyone. They kept the promise as well as George himself, who broke it three or four times more in the period named. One of the depositaries of the gruesome news was the guard who stood watch over the Deerfoot, while the owner and his companions went to the hotel to see that the hunger of the marooned young gentleman was appeased. This statement will explain the curious glances at the little group as they moved about the town, as well as the remark of the guard upon their return to the motor boat.

As night approached, George was impressed with his duty of acquainting the parents of Mike with the dreadful blow that had befallen them. They must hear of it sooner or later, and it was best that they should get it straight. Accordingly he motored thither, completing what I fear was not an unwelcome task in time to meet the Deerfootengaged on the same errand. Of course he heard the hail of Chester. He did not reply, for he was in no mood to make explanations and receive censure for what he had done from a high sense of duty—as the offender always insists in similar circumstances.

Everything was so plain to Alvin and Chester that throughout the conversation that followed their entrance into the home of Pat Murphy, they did not once ask the much afflicted parents of the source from which they had received their information.

The father was sitting in his chair at the side of the room bowed and silent in grief that was too deep for him to seek solace from his pipe. The wife sat on the other side of the room, rocking to and fro, flinging her apron over her face, the tears flowing down her cheeks, and her features twisted with anguish. So absorbed were they in their sorrow that they hardly glanced at the boys and did not address them.

Alvin could not restrain his sympathy at sight of the suffering of the couple, the father's none the less than the mother's because it was mute. The youth's promise to Mike was thrown to the winds and he called out:

"Stop your mourning! Mike hasn't been drowned!"

"Phwat's that ye say?" demanded the father, who half rising from his chair was staring at the lad as if doubting the words that had reached him. The wife, grasping each side of her apron with a hand and about to fling it upward, was equally quick in checking herself and with her mouth wide open she hoarsely exclaimed:

"Phwat! Say that agin!"

"Mike is alive and well as he ever was in his life."

They still stared, dazed and unable for the moment to speak another word. The callers sat down.

"I say again that Mike is well and safe. He spent last night on a little island not many miles away and we brought him back in the Deerfoot."

The mother still gazed and clutched her apron. Her husband showed that he caught the meaning of what he had heard.

"And where is Mike?"

The question recalled Alvin's promise to pave the way for his friend's return to his home.

"Before I tell you," said the Captain, "you must give me your pledge that you will not punish him for what happened last night. Will you do so?"

"That I will," was the unhesitating answer. "He desarves a licking, but we'll call it square—that is," was the qualifying condition, "so far as this thing is consarned."

"What! Lick me baby Mike!" exclaimed the glad mother; "not in a thousand years! Where is the darlint that I may kiss the hid off him?"

"Remember, Pat, what you just said. Mike isn't to be blamed for what took place and you should be as thankful——"

Just then a terrific crash was heard in the kitchen, the door to which was closed. The mother, in her highly wrought state, screamed and sprang to her feet. Her husband snatched up the candle from the stand in the middle of the room and ran to learn what the uproar meant, with his wife just behind him.

It seemed to be a night for the general breaking of promises. It will be remembered that Mike had agreed to stay on board the Deerfoot until he saw the door of his home opened by one of his friends and heard a whistle as notice that the path had been cleared and he might go forward. The two, however, had hardly entered the building when Mike changed his mind. With a refreshing forgetfulness of what he had lately passed through, he said:

"It's mesilf that is in danger of catching a cowld in my hid, as Larry McCarty said after slaaping in an ice box, and in stepping ashore, I may as well step a little furder."

Thus it came about that Alvin and Chester were no more than fairly inside the small house when Mike moved softly to the door and listened to the voices within. He was disappointed in not being able to distinguish everything said, though it will be recalled that no one spoke in whispers.

Suddenly it occurred to the boy that he could do much better if within the house itself. The darkness of the kitchen showed that the door connecting that with the sitting room was closed. He knew he could hear more plainly from the smaller room.

Being in darkness, he had to depend upon the sense of feeling. It was no trouble to raise the sash without making any noise. When lifted well up, the catch held it in place and he began crawling stealthily through. He saw the thin line of light under the door and heard what was being said on the other side. Knowing the room so well he needed no illumination to guide him. He balanced himself for a moment and then dropped lightly to the floor. More properly he tried to do so, but unaware of the chair in his way, he tumbled over that, which in turn tumbled over him, and caused the crash that startled those in the sitting room and brought his parents to learn what it all meant.

One glance at the sturdy figure struggling to his feet and muttering impatient exclamations told the mother who he was. Thrusting her husband aside, she rushed forward, straightened up the overturned chair, and dropping into it, seized her boy with both arms:

"Praised be! Me own darlint! Me baby! Bliss yer heart!"

She was striving frantically to pull him upon her lap and would have succeeded had Mike not been larger than she and strongly opposed to acting the part of an infant. There was good-natured strife between them for a minute or two, with the laughing father and two youths looking on. Then Mike triumphed, forced his parent upon one knee, and with an arm around her ample waist began bouncing her up and down with a vigor that broke her words apart, though it did not prevent her from grasping him about his neck and crying with joy.

"Arrah, mither, but it's yersilf that makes a fine barrel of jelly. Hist now! Can't ye sit still," he protested, bouncing her harder than ever.

Alvin and Chester held their sides, for it was the funniest spectacle upon which they had ever looked. By and by Mike released the happy victim, and all returned to the larger room, where they sat down. Alvin said:

"It's been fixed, Mike. The slate is wiped out up to this night. You and your father begin over again in the morning."

"Does he spake the thruth, dad?" asked the lad gravely.

"Alvin always does the same, but ye can make up yer moind ye'll be in my debt afore the morrow's night."

"I don't doubt it, as Barney Foord said whin he was voted the biggest fool in siven counties. Whisht!"

A timid knock sounded and Mike sprang up and opened the outer door. Mollie, one of the maids, stood smiling.

"There's a gintleman waiting fur ye at home," she explained.

"Waiting to see me?" repeated the surprised Alvin, rising to his feet.

"That's what he said and he will bide till ye returns."

"Well, good night, folks!" called Alvin to the happy family. "Come, Chester."

The two went out together, wondering who the caller could be. The brief distance was quickly traversed, and, passing through the front door, they turned into the handsomely furnished library.

As the lads entered, a man rose.

"You are Alvin Landon, I believe," he inquired, "and you," turning to his companion, "are his friend, Chester Haynes."

If ever two youths were astonished, when they made courteous reply to the salutation, they were our young friends, for the caller who thus addressed them was the man in gray that had followed them to the inlet on Barter Island and had now come to Alvin's home at Southport.

"If you can spare me a few minutes I have something of importance to say to you," he added as he took the seat to which Alvin waved him.

It proved an important interview indeed, but the revelation made by the man in gray and the events which followed there-from will be told in the second volume of the Launch Boys Series entitled "The Launch Boys' Adventures in Northern Waters."

THE END.

Made in the USA
Lexington, KY
31 July 2019